BOBBY TRANSFORMED

Blake Allwood

Cover designed by Samrat Acharjee

This book is a work of fiction. Names, characters, places, and incidents either are products of the author's imagination or are used fictitiously. Any resemblance to actual persons, living or dead, events, or locales is entirely coincidental.

Blake Allwood
Visit my website at www.blakeallwood.com

Printed in the United States of America
Box Elder, SD

First Printing: March 2020
Second Printing: March 2021

ISBN: 978-1-956727-06-7

Library of Congress Control Number: 2021919811

Titles by Blake Allwood:

Purchase at:
readerlinks.com/mybooks/4515

Join Blake's email list to get advance notice of new books and receive his occasional newsletter:
blakeallwood.com

Thank you to the following people for their assistance:

Louisa Keller – Developmental Editor
Kristopher Miller – Line Editor 1st Edition
Janine Cloud – Line Editor 2nd Edition
Dee Friloux – Proofreader
Julia Firlotte – Proofreader
Jo Bird – Copy Editor 2nd Edition

A special thank you goes to all my friends and family who supported me, I couldn't have done it without you.

And finally, an extra special thanks to my husband who continues to tolerate me, no matter how many of these rabbit holes I keep going down.

Bobby Devereaux

I need a damned job!" I screamed to the empty apartment before slumping in my chair.

It'd been another crappy day spent navigating New York streets, literally old-schooling it as I went from place to place asking potential employers if they'd gotten my resume. Hoping maybe since I was probably the only person physically showing up it might help me get my next journalism job.

I guess I'd gotten ten flat-out No's and a couple of nice guy Maybe's before I gave up and headed back to the apartment overlooking Central Park.

Randy was a drop-dead, gorgeous, wealthy trust fund baby I'd met just weeks after arriving in New York.

I was fresh off the farm and had a journalism degree from my tiny, private, midwestern college which had certainly helped me become a great writer but had done nothing to prepare me for living in one of the largest cities in the world.

I plopped onto the ridiculously expensive couch and opened my laptop. *Crap no power.* I quickly realized the dang power cord was dead.

I banged my head against the couch. "Damn It!" I yelled out loud again.

I closed my eyes and forced myself to breathe. I hadn't wanted to move in with Randy but when my sublet was up, he convinced me he wanted me to. "I have all this space and I want you to wake up in my arms."

God, I'm such a mushy pushover...

Randy also convinced me to go into this as an open relationship. Which honestly wasn't my way at all. I was a one man's man. But, apparently, I'm also a pushover...so I let him convince me. And now, here I was.

"Get a job, get your own apartment," I whispered. That had become my mantra since the paper who'd initially recruited me laid me off less than a year after arriving.

Randy and I could be a couple, but I wouldn't be mooching off him. A thought that caused my stomach to churn if I let myself contemplate it too much.

When I raised my concerns with Randy he just laughed and said, "Your midwestern hickish pride is just getting in the way. No one from here would care. Just enjoy it."

So, as was becoming too common where Randy was concerned, I pushed the discomfort away. I wasn't going to "just enjoy it," though, I was determined to find that job and get back up on my own two feet.

I looked over toward Randy's desk and knew he was out hooking up with some guy. I sighed, Randy never tried to hide it but even though we had an agreement, it still stung.

He'd clearly left shortly before I'd gotten back to the apartment since the screen on his laptop was still open. He'd also texted to tell me he'd be out most of the afternoon. I flipped open my laptop, and nothing happened.

I really needed to check my emails, just in case I'd got a job offer. It's New York, and the competition was fierce. If you let something slip, even for a moment, you could lose out on your one chance for a job.

I looked back up at Randy's laptop. It was open to Facebook of all the fucking things. I didn't even know he had a Facebook account. Seriously, he was a conspiracy theorist and would spout off for hours about how all social media was for was to spy on everyone.

Randy and I didn't really have an agreement about using each other's laptops. Truth was, it had never come up. But I assumed since knew almost everything about each other anyway, what could it hurt? Still, I probably should've closed his page before using the laptop. Good intentions aside, one of his messages caught my attention.

It was from some twinky-looking guy named Jessie. Okay, maybe not a whole lot different from me, except I had a bigger, more muscular frame. I was curious what kind of guy my man was fucking when he wasn't fucking me, so I opened the twink's profile to get a better look.

Within seconds he messaged me.

Hey, you still coming over?

I ignored it, knowing I was skating on thin ice.

Seriously, man, you got me all worked up. It's not fair to do that then leave me hanging. Besides, don't you want to get away from that mooching freeloader you got stashed up in your space?

I stared at the screen for several minutes, unsure what to think.

The next message prompted me to scroll through the rest of the conversation. Fuck decorum.

I thought you were gonna kick him out on his ass. When you do, I can come there and avoid all this headache.

The more I read, the more appalled I became.

Randy was trashing me left and right. He'd told the guy I was fat, sitting around all day doing nothing but eating his food. He even said I refused to look for a job.

But what really got me, and sent me into a massive tailspin, was that he'd told this twink I was so depressed I'd refused to shower for a week!

This was all such fucking bullshit! I looked for jobs every fucking day. When no one responded to my resumes, I started doing what I'd done today, which was physically knocking on doors. Sure, I'd been depressed right after I'd been laid off. Who wouldn't be, just a year after uprooting my life, navigating a huge cultural shock transitioning from middle-of-nowhere Iowa to one of the largest cities in the world, and then being dropped like a piece of trash? Despite that, I showered *every single* day.

Was I fat? I was certainly not as buffed up as I had been working on the farm, and at college I'd been friends with guys on the football team and worked out with them.

Was I as cut as I had been when Randy first met me? No. But that little twink he was talking to barely had any muscle on him at all. Why the hell was he telling someone I'd gotten fat?

It was all too much. I sat down in Randy's chair and wrote the twink back.

The freeloader will be out by five, then you and my ex can have the whole place to your fucking selves.

I pressed send.

It was liberating. Until that moment, I hadn't realized how much I didn't want to live with Randy in his pretentious apartment overlooking Central Park. I didn't want to ride another freaking subway in ninety-degree heat or smell the horrible stench of body odor every time I turned a fucking corner. I wanted to go home. Not that it'd smell better there, but at least it was the hogs that stunk and not hordes of people.

Despite my resolve and new feeling of liberation, my hands shook as I packed.

"Why did he talk me into moving in here?" I asked out loud.

It all felt like one of his conspiracy theories he liked to rant about, but this time, he was the one conspiring against me.

After I packed and put all the stuff I wasn't going to take with me out by the trash, I went back in to grab my bags, check for anything I'd forgotten and make sure the place was spic and span. I didn't want to give that fucker any reason to bad-mouth me. Not that anyone I ever met in the future would give a fuck what I did or didn't do or care what that bucket of hog slop thought or said about me.

In a final act of rebellion, I decided to leave a Post-it on his computer that said, "If you're curious why I left, read the message I sent to the dipshit you've been fucking."

By seven o'clock, I was on a plane. As I waited in the LaGuardia terminal, I reserved a hotel room near the airport in Des Moines where I'd spend the night. I didn't want to go back to the farm just yet. The first step was to survive the emotional backlash I figured was coming before I inadvertently exposed my parents to it.

When I finally landed and turned my phone back on, I'd gotten multiple texts from Randy.

"Idiot," I said under my breath.

One of the women walking by looked over, embarrassing me, but when she saw I was looking at my phone, she smiled. Fuck! I'd missed the Midwest. If I'd done that in New York, I'd have had to listen to someone ream me or been flipped off. Iowa might not have all the amenities of the big city, and I would miss the Off-Broadway shows I'd come to love, but there were more things I'd enjoy about being home.

I deleted Randy's messages without reading them. Deep down I honestly didn't give a crap what he had to say. I guess that said a lot about our relationship when that was all it took for me to get over him.

Not over the humiliation of what he'd said about me, that would take time. I wasn't quick to trust someone, so it hurt more than it should when they betrayed me.

When I got to my hotel room, I crawled into bed and instantly fell asleep. I woke up at five the next morning. Too early. I'd fully intended to sleep late, but I was still on New York time and I usually got up around six to start my workout routine. Six in New York was five in Des Moines.

Surrendering to my internal clock, I decided to make the most of it and crawled into the bathroom, then fumbled through my luggage until I found some gym shorts and a t-shirt. I made my way down to the tiny hotel gym and did about thirty minutes on the treadmill. When I came out, the receptionist smiled at me and said coffee was ready. I grabbed a cup to go and headed back to my room.

I figured the laptop would still be dead, but I was bored so I opened it anyway, just in case. To my surprise, it kicked on, although the battery was way low. I plugged it in and after whacking the damned cord several times, I managed to get it to charge.

I went through my emails, and of course, there were no offers. I wrote to a couple of friends who'd asked me what'd happened, telling them I was back in Des Moines.

Facebook had nothing that caught my attention. I closed it, looked at the clock, and moaned when I saw it was only six.

I set the laptop aside, making sure not to move the power cord. Seeing it was still charging, I sighed and lay down on the bed.

Since I was a little boy, any time I was upset I'd come up with elaborate stories in my head, turning people I was angry with into science fiction monsters. My parents had taken turns being evil dragons or soul-eating vampires. My brother and sister, of course, usually got the nastiest end of the stick as I'd imagine them as zombies or evil sorcerers. It sounds weird, but it relaxed me and made me feel more at peace. After long bouts of them going on killing sprees, the hero—always me, of course—saved the world from their malicious tendencies. Then I'd feel better and would be able to make amends.

I'd never told anyone. Besides, I hardly ever did it anymore. Well, until now.

When I closed my eyes, Randy transformed into a hideous monster who spewed venom at those who trusted him. The story spun through my head, becoming more and more outlandish as I lay there.

Inspired, I tried to remember the story, I began to write it down as a way to document the time I wasted on him, thinking I'd eventually read it to my friends. In my mind, I saw us sitting in our favorite bar, me reading the story, and them laughing their asses off.

In my mind I turned New York into a place where zombies who smelled like human excrement wandered around, trying to eat your brain. The entire thing was ludicrous, and I had more fun writing it than I'd had in a long time.

When I looked at the clock, it was almost ten.

Wow, where did the time go?

It'd been a long time since I'd been this inspired to write so I reserved the room for another day and let inspiration take me. Besides a quick workout the next morning, I wrote until I fell asleep late that night.

I woke the next day feeling a lot better than I should have after an insane writing jaunt. Eating the cardboard breakfast served by the hotel, I read over my document, made some tweaks then called my parents.

"Hey, mom," I said when she answered.

"Hey, yourself, how are you?"

"Well, how about I meet you for lunch and tell you all about it?"

The line was silent while she processed what I'd asked.

"Are you home?"

"I'm in Des Moines, and I'll be leaving for the farm in a few minutes."

She said she was excited to see me, but dang, she couldn't be more excited than I was. I'd come home and didn't have words to say how happy I was to be back in the part of the world where I belonged the most.

Two hours later, I pulled into the driveway of my parent's home in a great mood. Mom and Dad met me at the door and pulled me into a hug.

"So, are you going to tell us what happened?" Mom asked.

I sighed. I should've known she'd ask right away.

I had to stop myself from laughing at her directness. "Well, you know I was laid off and Randy talked me into staying in New York?" They both nodded. "I guess he really didn't want me after all. I accidentally saw something he wrote about me. So, when I figured out he didn't want me to stay, I flew home. Oh my God, I am so happy to be back!"

"What did he say about you?" Mom asked not letting me off the hook. I could see the indignation flowing out of her and again I had to stifle a laugh.

"Mom, it doesn't matter. He doesn't matter. I'm telling you, this really is for the best!"

My parents exchanged a worried look.

Straining to keep his voice calm and diplomatic, my Dad weighed in. "You seem to be taking this well." My father was a major defender of his family and there were a lot of unsaid things in that remark. It was good Randy was halfway across the country or I'm sure my father would've had words for him.

I shrugged off their mood hoping to convey how glad I was to be out of the relationship. "I know it sounds weird, but I realized the moment I read his hateful messages that I was done with him. I'm not really into the same things he is. I prefer the simple things in life. He's pretentious and loves his money. So, when I saw what he'd written, it sort of liberated me."

Both parents nodded, indicating I was finally getting through to them. "Baby, you're better off without him if he's like that. Do you need anything?" mom asked causing me to smile. I really did have the best parents in the world.

"Is my room still available or did Dad turn it into a man cave?" I asked, not really wanting to look into their concerned faces any longer.

"Not yet, but he's been threatening to," Mom teased as I walked up the stairs of the old farmhouse.

Long before I was born, my parents had built a fourth bedroom for themselves downstairs off the kitchen. The upstairs was now reserved for grandchildren or for me when I came home for a visit. I loved the idea of having the entire upstairs to myself. My older brother had taken over the operation of the farm, but he and my sister had their own homes and families now.

I flopped on my bed like I used to when I was a teenager. I had purchased a new charger on the trip home and pulled it out to plug my laptop in.

I opened my story and began reading from the top. I laughed through the whole thing, surprised at how I'd portrayed the people who'd been hateful or who were difficult to work with in real life.

I'd finished reading just as Mom called me down for supper and I decided to throw caution to the wind. My former coworker, Roy, and I had become close while working together. He'd been laid off the same day I was, but he immediately landed a job editing for a big publisher. We used to copy-edit each other's work, and now that he was editing fiction, I wanted his take on the story. I quickly sent him an email.

Roy,

Hey, I just finished this wacky novel and wanted your opinion on it. It's a rough draft, but maybe with a little editing I could self-publish? Anyway, if you have time, read it over and let me know what you think.

Bobby

I doubted I'd hear back from him anytime soon. The publishing house had inundated him with work the moment he was hired, but I knew he'd be honest with me. If it was shit, he'd tell me straight out.

I went down to dinner in an excellent mood, which of course, confused my parents even more.

"Sweetheart, I don't understand how you can be so nonchalant about this," my mom said, still looking concerned. "You can't have cared much about this man."

"Oh, leave him alone. He's a Deveraux, he'll be just fine." Dad raised his eyebrow. "Won't you, son?"

Before I could respond, mom hit dad on the shoulder with a dishtowel she'd used to bring the food out and said, "Bobby is and always will be my baby." She came over and kissed me on the top of the head. "Moms are entitled to worry."

Mom looked at me for a long moment with narrowed eyes. "Besides, I bet Bobby has something up his sleeve. He's never been one to just let something go."

I grinned, knowing my mother was going to figure things out soon. She always did know when something was going on with us kids.

I confessed that I'd written the book. As I described it to them, they alternately chastised me and laughed at my audacity.

"Bobby Franklin Devereaux, you were not raised to be so naughty," my mom said with fake indignation.

I winked at my dad, chuckled, and said, "You can't unlearn what you inherit naturally."

Dad guffawed. Mom was a practical joker and was always up to something. Which is probably why she could detect that same characteristic in us kids. If I was naughty, it was totally because I inherited it from her.

Liam Rickard

Crap. That's what they kept bringing me. Crap on top of shitty crap. My anger was whirling around me and getting more intense by the moment.

Rickard Publishing had only published three new books this month and sales had reached an all-time low.

"Because they're shit!" I said to the room and tossed a notebook into the air out of sheer frustration.

"Hey, you," I called from my desk, and my assistant walked in shaking. I'd completely forgotten the woman's name, but heck, she was my third assistant in the last month. I already knew she was on her way out as well.

Why did Mrs. Glendale have to retire? I asked myself for the hundredth time.

My dad's former assistant had been a tough old bird and gave back what I dished out. She never quaked in her boots.

I forced myself to calm down and knowing that my tall frame, which towered over most people in the office, was intimidating, I remained seated while I addressed her.

"I need to see the executives in an hour in my conference room. Tell them if they don't show, I'm firing the lot of them!"

She actually curtsied, God help me. But at least she'd get the worthless execs into my fucking boardroom so I could ream them all at once.

My father had stepped down as CEO of Rickard House Publishing a little over a year ago, handing the reins over to me. My grandfather founded the company over fifty years ago, but if I didn't produce something that hit the bestseller lists soon, the board would fire me from my own family's company.

The meeting did nothing to make me feel better. They proposed the same old crap.

After one of the lead editors, who was dry as a desert bone, proposed we do another romance. We'd produced two already this year and neither had gotten any traction. I sighed. "There are millions of writers out there trying to get published, even *self-publishing*, yet no one can find a single title that isn't reconstituted garbage?" I yelled.

When I looked around the room of blank faces, my temper snapped.

"What are you all doing with your time? Playing golf? Watching internet porn?"

The overpaid executives around the table squirmed, but not nearly enough to make me feel better.

"I want everyone from Acquisitions in the third-floor conference room at two today. Editorial, too. No, wait, I have a better idea," I said causing the executives to stop in their tracks. "Make it everyone on the payroll. Mandatory meeting, in the auditorium. No exceptions. Be there or be fired."

The group quickly scuttled out of my sight. They really were incompetent as hell. What was my father thinking when he'd put this group of clowns into these positions?

When they were all gone, I sighed. I knew this afternoon's meeting was going to be seen as a Hail Mary, and I was already bracing for the backlash the board was going to give me. I went back to my office, closed the door, and opened the first *Harry Potter* book, the *Holy Grail* of fiction.

It'd made millions upon millions appealing to adults as well as children. Nothing had come close to its sales since.

I didn't need to publish a *Harry Potter* series to be happy, I just needed something besides...well, besides shit.

I thumbed through the book, remembering the joy I'd experienced reading it as a child.

Like so many other kids, reading the Potter series was when I fell in love with books. That was when I became someone who'd eventually follow in my father's footsteps.

I set the book down and put my head in my hands. If this meeting didn't work, I was going to blow all the hard work I'd put in between reading the *Harry Potter* series as a child and now.

I arranged for upbeat music to be playing in the hall when the employees showed up. There wasn't enough room for everyone to sit, and technically we were going to be breaking fire code with everyone in one room, but I didn't need to talk for long.

When I walked onstage, the obligatory applause sounded throughout the hall.

Suck-ups, I thought bitterly to myself. But I gave a big smile anyway and waved at the crowd.

The music stopped and I picked the mic up.

"I know you're all confused about why I called you here today, but it's no secret that for the past few months we've struggled to find novels that touch the souls of our readers. It's time for that to change. I'm challenging you, as employees of Rickard Publishing, to find me the next great novel. If you read something that comes in, even if it needs a lot of editing, and it catches your attention, makes you smile, encourages you to read it to the end, step up and let your supervisors know. If they don't listen to you, and you really think it's special, email it directly to me."

I could see the crowd squirming. I knew this would cause some major heartache, so I lifted the *Harry Potter* book above my head.

"Twelve publishers turned down J.K. Rowling when she submitted *Harry Potter*." I let that statement drift through the hall and gave everyone a moment to think about it before I continued. "Twelve. That is a travesty of mountainous proportions. The next best novel is floating in the ether and waiting to be plucked out. It's possible we may have already turned it down. Well, not again, not now! Find that novel, and the person who brings it to their supervisor will get a bonus proportionate to the book's success."

There was a cheer as I walked off the stage. I could almost hear my father calling me an idiot, but when I'd inherited the company, it was already on the downward slide. I needed to make changes to keep up with the market. The company needed to attract a different kind of novel to kick us out of the free fall we were in or all our work was going to be for nothing.

Two days later, I got an email from one of our new editors. He had balls, going over his supervisor's head. As of yet he was the only one who had.

I opened the attached document, read it, and almost got a fucking hard-on. The story was a mixture of *Mad*

Magazine and Marvel Comics. It was awesome, funny, ridiculous in the best ways possible, and I was both smiling and tense at the same time.

The author's writing was raw, and most of the story would need to be rewritten. Still, there was a natural wit and underlying humor that, if edited correctly, would make readers want to read the story multiple times.

I had a strange desire to meet the author. That was unusual since I normally wanted to avoid authors like the plague.

I had assistant number four bring the new editor to my office.

"How do you know this author?" I asked him, forgoing pleasantries in my eagerness to acquire this unpolished gem of a book.

I watched the man, searching my mind for his name again, all the while assessing how he handled himself in my presence.

"I worked with him at my last job," he said, meeting my gaze without wavering.

Ron? Ray? No...Roy. That was it. Roy Letterman. My new best friend.

"How many people turned this down?" I asked.

Roy shrugged, which told me he didn't want to push his luck too much.

"Okay, I'm putting you on this. I want it edited and fast. Can you get your guy to do the changes quickly or will he drag his feet?"

Roy looked stunned.

"I-I don't know. I can ask."

"Wrong answer, Roy. The right answer is you'll go sit next to him until it's done. We need this finished and ready to publish right now."

"Isn't it supposed to go through some process?" he asked.

"Man, I'm your CEO. It just went through the process and we're gonna publish this. If you're not up to the challenge, let me know now."

Roy's face broke into a smile before he said, "I'm sure I can persuade him to make the changes quickly."

Bobby Devereaux

Roy called me and seemed to be having some sort of attack.

"Dude, I showed this to my boss, the fucking main boss, and he was all like, *'Go sit with him and get this ironed out. You can work on this fast, right?'*"

"Slow down, Roy. The manuscript I sent you, you showed it to your boss and they wanna work with me?"

"Yeah, they're fast-tracking it. But that means no delays. Can you work fast if I get you the edits?"

"Of course, what else have I got to do?" I asked sarcastically.

"Cool, I'll send you the story back in pieces. You've got some major edits to do so it reads more like a novel and less like something you wrote for *The Post*."

I chuckled. "You got my number. I already know I wrote it more like a journalist telling the story than a novelist." I sighed. "Okay, send what you can, and I'll get to it. Oh, and text me when you email it, so I know to check my email. Don't be gentle with me, Roy. If

I'm going to pull this off, I need someone who will help me make this good."

Roy sent stuff to me throughout the day and into the night. It took me longer than I expected to redo the edits.

Fuck, I thought, this is a lot tougher than you'd think it would be.

I know I'm a bit arrogant, but I always assumed fiction was so fluffy that it didn't really need much editing. As Roy ripped my story to shreds, I learned the hard way that this was at least three times more difficult than prepping an article for publication.

I mostly stayed in my room for the next three weeks, writing, rewriting, and cussing Roy out when he disliked the third rewrite. Then I had an epiphany and was finally able to put all the missing elements into the final draft.

When Roy finally said he thought we were finished, I hated everything there was to hate about the story. Of course, I loved it too, but God help me if I had to read the damned thing again anytime soon...

After that, it was radio silence. I was a nervous, itchy mess after putting so much of my time, energy, and, well, myself into the past three weeks. The silence from the publisher was deafening.

I'd barely seen my parents while I was working. They were intrigued at first by the offer, but during the time Roy and I were in the thick of it, they pretty much just avoided me.

I couldn't handle my nerves any longer, so I fumbled through my old clothes from high school, found some work clothes that still fit, and went out to the hog barns to help my brother. There was always one thing you could count on in a big farming enterprise, there was never a lack of work. At least if I kept busy, I wouldn't end up scratching my skin off in a nervous fit.

My brother Louis and his crew, all people I grew up with, had a blast giving me shit.

"So, the fancy New Yorker's slumming it in the hog pens." Erik, one of the workers I'd gone to high school with and had been hired after we'd graduated, said teasing me.

"Like you'd be able to find New York on a map, Eric," I retorted before flipping him off. That day, I flipped a lot of people off, but it was all in good fun. We even laughed as I told them about my bad experiences.

When most of the harder chores were done, we were hanging around talking while I continued reminiscing. Knowing the guys would get a kick out of it.

"I was so green," I said shaking my head at the memory. "I ended up living in one of the most expensive apartments in New York with no clue that it was." Louis laughed the hardest at that, although I knew for a fact that my brother would be even more clueless than me.

"I mean, I didn't know what a pricey condo was. It's not like they're mansions or anything. I went up to this guy's condo that overlooked Central Park, and I was like, 'nice view.' I mean, seriously, how was I to know it was one of the priciest condos in New York."

I was getting into the story now. "Oh, and for like three months, no one in New York would talk to me. I wondered if the hog shit smell had somehow followed me. Seriously," I said. "People seemed to be avoiding me for weeks after I got there." Several of them were laughing hard enough to cry at that.

When I told them about the breakup, they sobered a bit and I could tell they were sympathetic. I appreciated that. They were rough old farmworkers. It said a lot about them that they could listen to the gay brother talk about his breakup and still feel for him. However, when I told them I'd written a novel about it and shared the details, they were back to belly laughing.

In fact, as I described how I'd taken my ex and turned him into a villain that basically spewed toxic hog poo, Levy Henry, an old man who'd been working here longer than I've been alive, laughed so hard he almost fell into the hog pen, which was never a good idea. Many years ago, my great-grandpa had a heart attack and fell in. The legend was that the hogs ate him.

It was probably just a story my dad told to keep us on our toes. Regardless, we were all afraid of being taken down by the hogs and seldom worked them alone.

By the time the day ended, I felt like I'd contributed. Like I had given back to the people I loved. After a shower, I came down for dinner, knowing I still smelled like the barn. My sister, Clair, and her husband, Jason, were sitting in the dining room along with Frances, my brother's wife, their son, and my sister's twins. They were all waiting for us to finish up and join them.

"What's all this?" I asked.

My mother came over and kissed the top of my head, saying, "You finished your book and your brother got a free day of labor out of you, so we figured that calls for a celebration."

I chuckled. "Who said I was free labor?" I held my hand out to my brother and, after looking at it and then back up at me, he slapped his hand on top of it.

"You're family and eating for free, consider it a trade."

I stuck my tongue out at him as I used to when I was little, and the entire table laughed.

It felt so good to be home and sitting among my family like this again. Mom and Dad didn't do much farm work anymore and left to snowbird in Florida every fall. Nobody blamed them. Iowa had harsh winters and after my dad's heart attack, it was basically a matter of how they wanted to spend the rest of their lives.

Dad seldom went into the barns anymore. Hog farming was tough and had its ups and downs. You often had a hundred hogs ready for market and in the morning, when you loaded them, the price might be good, but by the time you were about to pull into the sale barn, the price could drop right out, leaving you penniless.

I looked around the room and couldn't help feeling proud of my family. They were amazing people. Clair was a high school teacher, and Jason worked for the county's extension office. Both my siblings stuck close to our parents and that was a relief since I, the youngest, had taken off to the wild blue yonder, AKA New York.

As I watched them joke and prod each other, I swore if there was a way and if I could help it, I'd never go hightailing it that far away again.

***

Two weeks after Roy and I had last spoken, I started getting emails from literary agents. Apparently, Roy was referring them to me. I hadn't heard whether they were going to accept my edited book yet, but the email Roy finally sent me explaining the referrals said the publishing house didn't work with individual writers. Roy explained that during the last decade, the publisher's board of directors had decided to work only through the writers' agents.

I'd heard time and again how difficult it was to get an agent. Hell, just how difficult it was to get someone to look at your book to begin with. So, this all felt a little surreal.

When I wasn't working with Louis in the barns, I sent emails and began interviewing the various agents. A guy about five years older than me caught my attention. He was a bit of a nervous wreck, but like me, he had a passion for all things fantasy.

Roy sent him a sample of my writing and he immediately began begging for more. The other agents' responses were more reserved, some I heard from even came off as condescending. I didn't write back to any of them.

Douglass A. Phillips was my guy. I hired him via a phone call and a flurry of signed documents were sent back and forth via email.

Doug was ecstatic. I learned later that he was being described as a new, fresh face in the biz. He had managed to survive a few years, barely scraping by, but in the past couple of years, he'd represented three fantasy novels that had been fairly successful. That's the only reason Roy had suggested him. Well, that and I suspected Roy had a secret crush on him.

After signing the contract, Doug finished reading the story and kept texting me all night about how awesome it was. Finally, after two o'clock, I started ignoring him since I'd promised my brother I'd help him load top hogs the next morning. As it was, I would only get four hours sleep. That wasn't really enough to deal with several hundred squirrelly, two-hundred-pound pigs.

I sucked down three cups of my mom's coffee the next morning and dragged my ass to the loading corral. My brother looked at me strangely. "What's wrong with you?"

"The agent I just hired kept me up all night texting me about my manuscript." I ran my hand over my face, trying to get some circulation going.

"That's great, little brother!" Louis grabbed me in a bear hug. I winced as he squeezed, given that he was a foot taller and about fifty pounds heavier. I winced with relief when he let me go.

I took after my mom's side of the family and was shorter than my brother and only a couple inches taller than my sister. It sucked that the rest of my family, including cousins, uncles and even aunts, were all taller than me.

At least I'd also inherited my mom's skin tone and didn't burn every time I walked out into the blazing Iowa heat. Our mom was part Puerto Rican. Her parents had moved to Iowa in the early 1960s as part of the whole hippie movement. Now, they were about as Iowan as anyone could be. I adored my Grandma Ramirez and missed my grandpa, who'd died while I was in high school. They'd been the grandparents who spoiled me rotten. My dad's folks were hard, Iowa people who, I thought, Dar Williams had so eloquently represented in her song *Iowa*, where she sang, "*We didn't mean to bother but rather stayed in our houses and burned.*" Or words to that effect.

We managed to get the hogs loaded and the driver hauled them off to the market. Because it ended up being a good price day, Louis was in an excellent mood.

I helped him clean up the loading dock and he took a moment to show me his and Dad's latest innovation. They were building a huge new lagoon that cost several million, which made my heart pound in my chest. That was a lot of money for our little operation to put out.

When I said as much, he nodded. "If it continues to work out, we'll make back double what we have in it in a few years."

Then he showed me the purification system. At first, I thought it was somehow pulling the waste out of the water. But before I could offer my concern and skepticism, Louis looked at me and laughed.

"It's methane gas," he said. "We're purifying methane gas and selling it out west."

I looked over toward the little wooded area beside the lagoons and when I saw the yellow tag standing up, I asked, "Is that part of the gas line that runs through the property?"

My brother smiled. "Yep, we're building a system that'll allow us to feed the purified methane right into the line."

My great-grandpa, the one who was allegedly eaten by the hogs, threw a massive fit when they'd first run the line through his property, but he'd been overruled by the state and had to tolerate the damned thing. They did have to pay him for the use of the land, and that had ultimately helped save the farm. Now it seemed my brother and father had found a way to use it to their benefit.

"This is cool, but it's sort of risky, isn't it?" I asked.

"Yep, but brother, it's do or die. Like always," he sighed. "The hog market has been depressed since I took over. Pork prices have stubbornly stayed low since the latest economic crash."

Louis shook his head and I saw the same concerned expression on his face that I'd seen on my father's face throughout my childhood. "We can't keep surviving with the volatile agricultural markets unless we have a back-up plan. We know the folks who have started a similar enterprise in Missouri and seeing their success, we decided to go for it."

"You borrowed money?" I asked.

He shook his head. "No, but we pretty much cleaned out the slush fund."

I sighed deeply, clapped my brother on the back, and said, "I hope to God it works, brother."

He chuckled. "Don't we all?"

By noon, I was done helping him around the farm. After showering, I climbed into bed and fell asleep. I'd forgotten how much work farming involved. It had been easy to get a few hours' sleep, then get up to run around New York, interviewing, talking to sources, and even writing as long as you had enough coffee. But when you were down on your sleep, the physical labor of working on the farm was difficult, to say the least. I was happy I'd chosen a career where I could work with my mind and leave the farm management to my older brother.

By the time I woke up, it was almost dinnertime and I'd gotten a text from my friend Carla asking if I was available that evening to visit. Her twins were spending the night at their grandparents' house. Her mom had her other kids and her husband had to work late, so she had the night off.

I texted back saying,

Hell, yeah!

And we agreed to meet at the tiny bar in town we used to go to when she and I were on break from the University.

Carla was six feet tall and she had an even taller twin brother who I used to lust after. They were second-generation immigrants. Their parents moved to the US from Sweden and both had blond hair and blue eyes. They were beautiful inside and out.

Carla taught school with my sister Frances. Frances had put in a good word for Carla, and I'm guessing that was a big reason why she got the job. The two were great friends now, both having twins about the same age. I think Frances also leaned heavily on Carla to figure out how to raise twins so both kids felt loved.

We met at the bar and threw back a couple beers as we got reacquainted.

After spending a few minutes catching up, I could tell my friend loved her life, and I was happy for her. I was just a little envious that she had the life she wanted while I was still floundering.

She must've picked up on my thoughts because she sat up and said, "Oh, I'm such a bad friend. I'm sorry. Here I am going on and on about my life and you've just broken up with your boyfriend."

I smiled. "I'm not upset about breaking up with him. He was a loser. I'm just jealous you've got the life you've always wanted and a husband that adores you even after, what, four years of marriage? Hell, Randy and I had only been living together for a few months and he was already fucking other men more than me."

She shook her head.

"Men can be such total shits," she said. "Well, you're better off without him. But let's fix you up while you're in town. Our new principal is a hottie and rumors are that he plays for your team."

She wiggled her eyebrows and I reached over to playfully thump her on the head like I used to when we were in school.

"What? You don't wanna chase a hot gay high school principal?" she asked.

"How old is he?" I asked.

"Well, maybe thirty-five or so."

"Or so?" I asked and she laughed.

"Okay, he's probably closer to forty, but older men make better lovers," she said.

"Whatever. I'm not against dating older men. I'm just against dating *any* man at the moment. I'm happy to let things ride a bit until I'm more settled. On a different subject," I was feeling shy about tooting my own horn too much. Maybe because I was still afraid everything would fall apart, but also because I didn't want to sound boastful. "I finished editing my book and even have an agent."

"Really? That's so exciting! You're gonna be a rich author," she exclaimed.

"No, authors make shit. Unless they turn your book into a movie or something insane happens with your sales. But being a published author could help me in my other writing career."

"What do you plan to do?" she asked her excitement dying down.

I shrugged, thinking about trying to get a job at the *Des Moines Register* or maybe even one of the little papers still surviving around here. Although I didn't know if I'd be able to make a living that way.

"I guess I could always work for my brother."

Carla scrunched up her nose.

"Pig farmer? I have a hard time seeing you pull that off for the next thirty years," she said.

"Well, it's not like my family hasn't been doing it since Iowa was first settled," I replied. "It's in my blood, so to speak."

"It's on your skin too, but I wasn't gonna say anything."

I flipped her the bird, but I figured she was probably right. *Oh well, welcome to Iowa.* I thought.

"Do you wanna be a pig farmer?" she asked, serious this time.

I shook my head. "I don't mind helping out when I'm home, but no, it's not my thing. I never really did like it when I was growing up. My dad would force us all to help him, but I preferred to be in the kitchen helping Mom, to be honest."

"Oh, the life of a farmer," Carla sighed. "We do what we gotta, not what we wanna."

We spent the rest of the evening laughing at each other and catching up with our adult lives. I genuinely enjoyed Carla, and just being here with my dear friend confirmed I'd done right by coming home.

By nine o'clock, Carla was fading. I had a lot of fun picking on her about getting old before her time.

"You try having twin toddlers and teaching a bunch of high school hooligans all day and see how long you last!" she countered.

We hugged goodbye and set up a time for me to come over to her house for supper. I looked forward to it. Her husband Derek was sort of wacky and it was impossible to spend time with him without laughing so hard you were in danger of peeing yourself. They were so good together. As she walked out, I thanked God she'd found such a good match and briefly wondered if I'd ever be so lucky.

Liam Rickard

I was being overly cautious. If I hadn't known the author was currently sitting on a hog farm in middle-of-nowhere Iowa, I'd have been more concerned about someone snatching the book out from under me. But I was more afraid of flopping on another crappy novel.

After sending the manuscript to a confidential panel of readers and getting glowing reviews, I had the lawyers draw up an offer and sent it to the agent.

The response came back within an hour with a laughing emoji attached. "You've got to do a hell of a lot better than this."

"Well, that arrogant little shit," I said out loud.

I'd met Doug Phillips at various functions and although he was a lot to handle, I liked him. Not enough to date him, though. And right at the moment, I'd have loved to hit him in the nose. But he was right, I'd deliberately lowballed the offer. It was policy to try to get a good deal, especially with a first-time author stuck in the middle of nowhere. I thought we'd get a good deal on this one, especially considering we'd referred the agent to the new author in the first place.

I had the attorneys rewrite the offer and sent the update to Doug.

Two hours later, I had his response. No surprise, he asked for everything under the sun, so I sent our final offer, one which was more than generous but also protected us if the book wasn't successful. It was accepted within the hour, signatures all in place.

I did a happy dance and invited Irene, my latest assistant, in for a Champagne toast. Irene Edness was a Caribbean transplant, powerhouse of a woman, which she had made quite clear during her interview. She'd told me she knew all my other assistants had run away crying but that she wouldn't put up with my bullshit. If I hired her, I needed to be willing to deal with someone who could handle herself. I had been impressed and hired her on the spot, sending all the other applicants away.

She was exactly what I needed. The week she'd been working for me had been excellent. She certainly kept the place in order. She also seemed to have an innate skill of knowing what was important and needed my immediate attention and what could be held off until later. Because of her, my life became much more efficient and easier to manage.

She reminded me of my dad's assistant. The rest of my staff were afraid of her, which meant she could wrangle them when I was busy, keeping everyone in line for me. I was in love.

"If I weren't gay," I told her one day. "I'd ask you to marry me!"

She told me I was nuts but smiled as she walked out of my office.

Even if I hadn't just closed a deal on a book I was confident would be a big win for us, I would've been happy to open the hundred-dollar bottle just to celebrate hiring Irene.

I got the marketing team working, intent on getting the book out sooner rather than later. Usually I liked to build excitement, creating a larger audience before we released, but I didn't have that kind of time. The board was meeting for the final quarter, and if I didn't bring something of value to the table, I was going to be beheaded.

Ignoring the old saying about putting all your eggs in one basket, I put as much energy into Devereaux's book as I could. I was convinced Vortex Prism, the title we'd settled on, would be a major success but equally terrified that it wouldn't.

Luckily, my instincts had been correct and within weeks of the release, we started seeing the telltale signs of success. The news of the story spread through the fantasy community like wildfire. We already had an invitation for Devereaux to speak at the next Comic-Con in New York the following February and I'd been personally contacted by a movie studio to discuss a movie deal. Those were two very significant wins and ones I hadn't expected to happen so fast.

I called Roy and asked him to have Doug meet me for lunch to talk about sending Devereaux on book tours and signings.

I'd given Roy two consecutive promotions. Mostly, I wanted him to replace the idiots who'd turned this manuscript down. It was my intention to start finding those who were more with it regarding the types of books that were selling today. I was tired of only crap landing in the decision committee's lap, and that meant reorganization from the bottom up.

Devereaux was a sensation. Especially after he and Doug recommended we begin working up a graphic novel version of the story to present during Comic-Con. Its release would surely catch even more of the millennial fantasy crowd's attention.

We'd never done a graphic novel, and I was a little lost. But Roy, who was proving himself to be a real asset, connected us with several graphic designers who were good but still trying to make a name for themselves.

We found a young woman, who was super smart and talented, to take on the project. Her art was perfect for Devereaux's story, serious and genuine while also maintaining Devereaux's humor.

Devereaux took on the writing for the graphic novel elements, cutting the novel down into bite-sized pieces, which made me love him even more.

When Comic-Con burst open, the graphic novel outsold the book ten-to-one. We were off to the races.

I had yet to meet this author, mostly because we were never in the same place at the same time. I had thought several times that I should try to figure out a way to meet him, and that became even more important because by the end of the first year, despite a movie deal, the book sales were beginning to fall off. I'd been putting a lot of pressure on Doug to get Devereaux to write a second novel. But no matter what we offered, the author refused.

I'd kicked myself repeatedly for not making that a requirement in the contract, or rather for not sticking to my guns and keeping it in the contract when he'd balked at it initially. It was easy to forget how under-the-gun I'd been at that time, and I tried desperately not to remember.

After discovering we were getting better revenues from fantasy audiences, I began reorganizing our company's focus. In fact, we tried to stay within the same genre as *Vortex Prism*, and although we'd published some good books and graphic novels, however, we'd yet to hit the same success as we'd had with Devereaux's book.

After some tedious arguments with Doug and even putting pressure on Roy to encourage his friend to give us a part two, I decided I was either going to have to give up or kick down his damned door.

It wasn't really in my nature to give up, so I booked a flight to Des Moines, fully intending to make this man see reason.

Bobby Devereaux

I was tired. I had never intended or planned for the book to be a success. The fact was I wrote it to help me process my breakup with Randy, something to make my friends and family laugh at my awkward experiences in the Big Apple. But people ate it up from the moment it hit the bookshelves.

I was bored with the book within weeks of it coming out, so I suggested turning it into a graphic novel. It was a good suggestion since that increased sales exponentially.

The problem was I figured out that I didn't really see myself as a fiction writer. I loved Comic-Con, but I didn't really enjoy the book tours that ate up most of my summer and I sure as hell didn't want to sign another fucking graphic novel as long as I lived.

I was so thankful that I'd had the sense to refuse to write another book, even though they cut my initial check in half. At the time, it had felt harsh, but now I waved it off. I had enough money sitting in the bank from the royalties, and with the upcoming movie planned to come out just over a year after publication, my account would almost double. I wasn't set for life by any means, but I sure as hell could take my time finding the job that was right for me.

I'd begun checking out jobs as a reporter for various publications. I was even playing with the idea of doing location work, which would allow me to travel but when each assignment was done, I could come back home to Iowa.

After the summer of book tour hell, I bought the little farm next to my parents when it came up for sale. The old farmhouse had stood vacant for years since the widow who owned it had developed dementia and moved into a nursing home. Thirty acres came with the farm. I didn't need or want that much land, but it was good cropland and my brother was salivating at the thought of being able to grow corn and soybeans to help offset the cost of feed. Being savvy enough to think before donating it to him, I forced my brother to agree to help me renovate the home as a trade for using the fallow land.

The homestead was rustic even after we were done working on it, but it was good enough for me to live in. And if I were going to be gone more often than not, I just needed the basics anyway. My parents were upset that I wasn't staying with them, especially since they would be gone most of the winter. But I knew my brother wanted to move his growing family into the house so he'd be closer to the operation. Mom and Dad weren't quite ready to give up the home they raised us in, but I thought the smaller ranch house my brother and his wife lived in, which had belonged to my grandparents when they retired, was a better bet for them. I knew they saw that too, but it was still hard for them to give it all up even when they were gone a third of the year. Regardless, I didn't want to be the reason why they didn't move out and let Louis move in.

The furnace in my new place was shot and even though it was only the first week of October, the temperature outside was cold as all get-out. I had turned on an electric heater I borrowed from my folks to keep my pipes in the basement from freezing, but the upper floors were still too cold to be comfortable.

I had several books to sign and send back to Roy, as well as some paperwork to get caught up on. I didn't want to haul it over to my parents for the night. Besides, I didn't trust the old electric heater to stay on and I wanted to keep an eye on it.

I needed to get the wiring redone as well as install the new furnace, but the only HVAC guy for miles around was dealing with a death in the family and said he couldn't get to me until the following week. That was one of the problems of living in such a sparsely populated area. Still, at least I knew the guy was going to give me a fair price when he finally got around to it.

The electricity was so bad I couldn't have the heater on and use anything else without throwing a breaker. I'd turned the heater off long enough to microwave a pizza, rushed back down to turn the heater back on, and was about to dig into my pizza when the doorbell rang.

"Dang!" I said out loud. "I didn't even know I had a doorbell."

When I opened the door, I recognized the man immediately. It was Liam Rickard, the CEO of Rickard Publishing and a total pain in my ass.

Surprised, I said, "Mr. Rickard, to what do I owe the pleasure?"

He shivered and came in without being asked. I closed the door behind him as he began taking layers of clothing off.

I laughed. "I wouldn't if I were you, the heat's out."

He looked at me strangely. "The heat's out? Why don't you call a repairman?" he asked.

I cocked an eyebrow.

"Why golly gee, I wish I'da thunk of that!" I said in my most pronounced hillbilly twang.

The man stared at me like I was an imbecile.

"Mr. Rickard, I'm going to ask again, why are you at my home in the middle of rural Iowa?"

He drew a breath and launched into what was clearly a prepared speech.

Two minutes into it, I sat down on my sofa. I wished to God almighty that I had popcorn to eat as I watched him.

He sputtered on for another minute or so. Some bullshit about living up to my potential, which I'd long ago stopped listening to. Now I was judging his face and body. He had a pleasantly round face, dark features on an otherwise light complexion. He had nice lips, and I wondered if he was a good kisser. Did he use those lips to their full advantage? Or was he more like Randy, who'd been good at first but then was too lazy to work at it as time went on?

He finally wound down and I said, "Wanna piece of pizza? It's gonna get cold."

He stared at me as I pulled the pizza out of the microwave, cussing to myself when I discovered it was indeed cold. I wasn't willing to go back down to the basement to turn the heater off again, so I just cut it up and brought it to the table.

"Sorry. It's already cold but help yourself."

"Did you hear anything I said?" he asked.

I shrugged. "A little bit, but it's all stuff you had your minion lecture me about before. Which I resent, by the way. Roy was my minion before he was yours."

I teased, causing the New York executive to blush with frustration.

Score! I thought, enjoying this a little too much.

He surprised me when he plopped down on my ancient side chair, grabbed a piece of cold eighty-eight-cent freezer pizza, and shoved a bite into his mouth.

"This stuff is shit," he said with his mouth full, causing me to laugh.

"Yep, but it does the job when your electric is also on the blink."

He looked around, shoving another bite of the crappy pizza into his mouth.

"Why do you live in such a rat hole?" he asked.

"Hey, it's not a rat hole," I said pouting before I caught myself. "I just bought it. She's a work in progress."

"If you say so. With what we're paying you, you'd think you could tear it down and build a new one."

"What you're paying me?" I asked. "If I remember right, I did all the work. You're the one scalping me here."

The man's eyebrow went up. I could tell he wasn't used to being talked to like a normal human being. Shit, people like him probably had people paid to fall at his feet, kissing them and using their lips to shine his shoes. Too bad. He picked the wrong guy if he thought I was going to do that.

He looked around the place again. I could tell he wanted to make another deprecating comment, but he held his tongue instead, saying, "Mr. Devereaux, I've come all this way to convince you to reconsider book two. That first book was perfect. It caught the attention of millions. Don't you want to do that again?" he asked.

I shrugged. "Nope, not really," I replied as I grabbed another piece of cold pizza and stuck it in my mouth. "I told both Doug and Roy that I'm done. I'm not sure what they said to you to encourage you to come all the way out here, but I know and *like* them. I'm not sure why you thought *you'd* be able to convince me."

He squinted at me when I said the word *like*, fully taking the bait. To his credit he didn't respond, although I knew he wanted to.

He took another piece of the bad pizza. I assumed he was trying to relate to me, which almost made me burst out laughing. I doubted he knew I was the ex-lover of Radford "Randy" Lupine, New York Billion-Dollar Trust Fund Baby. I knew what the New York Elite lifestyle was like and I knew it was stupid as shit. I also knew he wouldn't be trying to relate to me over cheap pizza if he knew. I decided to have a little fun with him anyway and let him continue eating while I amused myself.

"Tell me what I need to do to get you to write the next novel." He pulled his checkbook out then and began writing me a check. "How much would it cost to renovate this piece of..." He cleared his throat, which almost caused me to crack up again. "This nice home of yours?"

God, this was hard, I thought as I closed my eyes and put my hand over my face to hide the smile. When I'd composed myself, I looked him in the eye.

Hoping I could pull it off without laughing, I began speaking with a real country dialect. "I figure if'n yer willin' ta help me and mah folks tomorrah wid some work, it might'n help free up some time."

A glimmer of hope crossed his pretentious face and I almost, *almost* felt guilty for what I was about to do to the poor man.

He stuck out his hand for me to shake, and I reached over and took it. *Oh, fucking A, this was going to be mean, but oh so very much fun.* I suggested he go back to a hotel for the night and come back to the house to meet me tomorrow morning at six.

"You mean the town that's like thirty minutes back there?" he asked, pointing the wrong way. "Don't you have room here? Especially if you're gonna drag me into work tomorrow at six."

I smiled. "Dude, I don't have any heat. It's Iowa, it gets cold."

He shrugged. "I can handle cold if you can."

I hadn't intended to let him spend the night. I almost called over to my parents' house to see if they could put him up, but his arrogance was beginning to get to me. Did he just assume I'd fall at his feet and put him up when he showed up at my house uninvited?

"*C'est la vie,*" I said, then took him up to the guest room.

It still had the old mattress that had been there when I'd bought the place. I found some clean sheets and helped him make the bed, with no idea whether it would be comfortable. I'd bought the house furnished and I hadn't even been in the guest room more than once to see what was in here.

I gave him the Wi-Fi password, which shocked him. He clearly hadn't expected me to have Wi-Fi. Then, I left him to his own devices.

I went back downstairs, wrapped a blanket around me, and began signing books. About an hour later, he came down and asked if there were any food places we could order from. "I haven't eaten all day except for your um...pizza."

I just laughed. "Nope. If you're hungry, though, I could ask my mom if they have leftovers."

He shook his head and said, "I'm fine."

I felt bad for the arrogant ass. I'd always been taught how important hospitality is, more for yourself than for the guest. "*Never let someone go hungry,*" that was the farmer's motto.

"I have a casserole my mom made and froze for me. I'll heat it up."

"Seriously, I'm good," he said.

"Bullshit, you wouldn't have asked if you weren't hungry."

I went to the freezer and pulled the casserole out, tossing it into the gas oven. I turned the dial to four hundred fifty degrees and went back to my book signing.

"You do all those yourself?" he asked when I picked up another book.

I looked over at him. "Well, duh, I'm the author. Who else is gonna sign them?"

He shrugged. "I don't know. I just assumed you all hired an assistant with similar handwriting."

I looked at him aghast. "That's horrible, not to mention unethical. They don't want an assistant's signature. They want the author's and I don't know one author who does that. What's wrong with you? And why don't you already know that as the CEO of a publishing company?"

He shrugged and sat across from me. "Want me to do some?"

"Fuck no! Don't you have a secretary to harass or some exec to scare the shit out of?"

He looked at me funny, which was becoming a theme of this bizarre visit. "I don't scare my execs," he said.

I *did* burst out laughing at that one. "Dude, you know I've been working closely with the people in your company, right? I know how you are. They all call you a monster."

"That's all for show," he said defensively.

I looked up at him and realized that he really didn't think he was a bad boss. He truly believed the gossip was just for show.

I shrugged. It wasn't my place to give the guy a reality check. Besides, I was afraid I'd put Roy and the other folks I worked with at Rickard Publishing at risk if I pushed too far. Liam was a horrible man, by all accounts. The only person who could do anything with him was his latest assistant, Irene Edness.

"So, you're really gonna consider this book if I help tomorrow?"

"I said I'd *consider* it, but I'm not making any promises. Your best bet would be to go home and find another sucker. One who actually wants to be a novelist."

"*Sucker*? Why do you say that?" he asked. "We've treated you more than fairly with your contract."

"It's not about the contract or the money. It's about feeling good about what you're doing. I like writing, but all I've done since I wrote *Vortex* is run around trying to help your publishing company create a fake image that doesn't really represent who I am. I don't want an image. I'm a simple man and I like simple things. Think of me more like one of the old reporters from the smoky movies of the 1970s. Happily miserable but making a difference."

He choked at the reference, and I was about to lay into him for it when the timer went off.

I went into the kitchen, pulled the casserole out, and put it on top of the stove. I left the oven open, enjoying the heat.

Liam came over and took the fork from me, surprising me by tasting it straight from the pan.

"Damn, this is good. What is it?"

"My mom's the cook. It's some Puerto Rican thing she knows about, mixed in with a little Midwest flair."

We both ate standing up while enjoying the stove's radiant heat. I knew better than to leave a gas stove burning with the door open for long, but it sure felt good while it lasted.

When we'd both eaten our fill, we went back into the living room so I could finish signing the last few books and get to bed. It was fun for a minute, but now the guy was wearing on my nerves.

"You don't like me, do you?" he asked.

"I don't know you, so I can't answer that."

"But you don't have a good impression of me."

I looked at him. Stopping the pretense, I just said what I was thinking. "Anyone with any decency wouldn't just show up at a person's house to harass them into doing something they didn't want to do, and then expect them to offer him a room for the night."

He looked at me funny again, and I wished I was playing a drinking game where I could throw a shot back for every time I got that look. I was sure that being drunk with his sexy highness sitting in my cold, dilapidated home would've been a lot more fun than this.

I signed the last book, found the packaging Roy had given me to transfer them between New York and here, and packed the books up so they'd be safe.

The man watched me the entire time, not even pretending to look at his phone.

When I was done, I decided to ignore the paperwork for now. Even though it was still only nine o'clock, I went upstairs, found a few extra blankets my mom had brought over and put them on the end of his bed.

"We'll be up early tomorrow morning. I suggest you get some sleep," I yelled down. Then I went to my room, not worrying about what he would do for the rest of the night.

Liam Rickard

I went upstairs shortly after Bobby disappeared, assuming we were done for the night. I almost covered his casserole and turned off the lights, but it was going to be colder out here than in his refrigerator, and if he didn't mind about his lights, who was I to worry?

I knew showing up unannounced was presumptuous, but to be honest, any other author would've been honored, if not a bit overwhelmed, by my showing up on their doorstep. Clearly, I misread this one. As I lay on the ratty bed, I had to think he'd put me here on purpose to teach me a lesson. I also thought about how different he was from the other authors I'd worked with in the past.

I enjoyed watching him work. He was so beautiful. The pictures hadn't done him justice. He could've been a movie star if he wanted. His frame was thicker than a runner or swimmer, but not overly muscular or big, just well built.

As he moved around on his sofa, I could see indications of just how muscular the guy was. More than once I wanted to make a pass at him, just to see if I could get him to remove that shirt so I could taste what was underneath.

It was no secret he was gay, and he'd dated a bigwig New York City guy, although for the life of me I couldn't remember who it was. Story went, the guy was fooling around, and Bobby dumped him.

Since then, there had been no word of Bobby dating anyone seriously, and I knew from the fan mail that came to our offices that there were more than a few men who'd volunteered.

He wasn't entertained by me, and I'd always been able to ride on my position to get me by. When it became clear that wasn't something he cared about, I was at a loss as to what to do or say. I wasn't good with social graces. Even when I was in college, I tended to ride on my family name and didn't have to do much to impress people or make friends. I was the captain of the football team too, so I'd been thrust into a position of authority early on.

Something about a man who saw through all the filters intrigued me and made me horny as hell. I considered jacking off, but I didn't have a towel and didn't want to use my sock. So, I just turned over, trying to find the least uncomfortable part of the bed, and willed myself to fall asleep.

The next morning, I heard a tap on my door, and when I looked at the clock it was five-thirty. I was usually up before then in New York, but I hadn't slept worth crap on the old mattress.

"Time to get ready, sleeping beauty. Lots of work to get done."

I sighed. I'd agreed to this, and if it got him to write...well, so be it. It *would* be worth it.

I threw on the suit I'd worn the day before and came down the stairs. When I got to the bottom, I looked straight into a huge smile. The look on his face made me want to whimper. I hadn't had coffee or built up my resistance to such a pretty face this early in the morning.

"You seriously can't go work in a hog pen wearing an Armani suit."

"Hog pen?" I asked, still in a total slump and too tired to register everything I was hearing.

He laughed.

"Yeah, a hog pen. A really big one." He paused, looking me over again. "Well, come on. I'm sure we can find some work clothes for you at the farm."

I followed him out to his truck and climbed in, dozing as he drove the short distance. We pulled up to a farmhouse that looked similar to the one we'd just left, but this one appeared to be in significantly better shape.

When we walked in, I immediately smelled coffee layered with bacon and...was that biscuits?

Bobby sat me down at a huge table and introduced me to his mom. I stood back up and shook her hand.

"Mom, can you caffeinate this clown while I go find him some clothes that are appropriate for a real day's work?"

She smiled. "Mr. Rickard, what do you put in your coffee?"

"Whatever you want, just as long as it has caffeine in it."

She laughed again and brought me a cup, sugar bowl, and a small cream pitcher filled with what appeared to be real cream.

I poured in nearly all the cream and almost purred when the warm creamy mixture finally slid into my system.

"You are a real goddess for making nectar so sweet," I said, and she cocked her eyebrow at me in a funny way.

"You hungry?" she asked.

I shook my head.

"Not yet. I didn't sleep much and I'm a little nauseous."

She looked concerned.

"You know what you're doing today, right?" she asked.

I shrugged. "Doesn't matter to me if it'll get your son to write again."

She shook her head. "Ever been on a hog farm before?"

I shook my head.

"No, but I smelled it from the road. I'm guessing it's gonna be fun," I said sarcastically.

She sighed. "Well, for your sake, you better figure out how to get rid of that nausea or you're gonna lose whatever you've still got in your stomach."

"Oh, we had your casserole last night, it was really good. But what was it?" I asked.

"The one I made Bobby?" she asked.

I nodded.

"*Pastelón*, or a version of it. There are a lot of the traditional ingredients you can't get in this part of Iowa, so I improvised...or I should say my mom improvised. I just adopted her recipe."

"Whatever you did, it was delicious."

She smiled.

"I like you, and because I do, I'm going to help you out."

She went into the kitchen. When she came back out, she had a biscuit with butter and jelly on top. She brought it to me and said, "Eat all of this, even if you don't want to. Trust me, you need something on your stomach." She disappeared around the back of the kitchen into what appeared to be an annex. Then she came back with Zofran and handed me one. "You'll need to take this too. It'll help your nausea."

I swallowed the pill and ate the biscuit. When I was tossing the last bite into my mouth, Bobby came back carrying some ugly yellow overalls and a beat-up jersey of some kind.

"I think these'll fit. They're well-worn, but it's all we've got."

As he came near, I smelled the stench coming off the clothes. Despite the Zofran, I almost puked then and there.

Bobby looked at me, amusement written clearly on his face, which put my back up. I took the smelly coveralls and carried them at arm's length to a powder room on the first floor, where I removed my suit and pulled the crappy clothes on.

When I came back out, I left my suit hanging over the back of a sofa since Bobby's mom hadn't returned to tell me where to put it.

"Your mom okay with me leaving my suit there?" I asked.

He shrugged. "I'm guessing it won't be there long."

I squinted, sure now that I'd do whatever had to be done to survive this and show the arrogant asshole that I was made of stronger stuff than he thought.

When we finished eating, we went out the back door and toward a huge, long barn, its smell becoming more intense the closer we got.

Men moved around all over the place, and when they saw me, they looked surprised. After the surprise, a look of mischief crossed their faces.

A tall, rugged version of Bobby came up and shook my hand, telling me he was Louis, Bobby's older brother.

"You and Bobby are on washdown duty. I need you to clean down the house."

Sounded easy enough, or so I thought until Bobby escorted me into the building. I honestly couldn't breathe. The smell of ammonia was overwhelming, and we hadn't even gotten to the area where the pigs were yet. He watched me while I caught my breath and I was thankful I hadn't vomited right then and there. I silently thanked Bobby's mother for the Zofran.

When Bobby was confident I wasn't going to puke, he handed me a set of waders. He took another set for himself and pulled them on, quietly showing me how it was done.

With the horrible smell it was hard to exert effort and breathe at the same time, and I finally asked, "Shouldn't we have a gas mask on or something?"

Bobby chuckled.

"You'll get used to it soon enough." Then under his breath he added, "If you last that long."

I stared a hole into his back, pissed he was enjoying this as much as he was.

When we came into the main room, the hogs were everywhere. Wire crates housed individual animals and they were all making noise at the same time. The noise combined with the smell was almost unbearable. Bobby handed me a hose and took one himself, spraying the hog shit into canals built along the outside of the cages.

I sighed, made the mistake of breathing through my mouth, and almost choked. I caught my breath and began spraying the poo toward the canals too. Before long, we managed to get the poo cleaned up in the pen and shortly after, more men came in to do the rest.

I followed Bobby to the entrance room again and we removed the waders. I still hadn't gotten used to the smell, but it wasn't as bad as it had been when we first came in. Being back out in the air was like being liberated after being buried underground.

Louis came toward us. "Hey, Bobby!" he yelled when he was still several feet away. "There's been a spill over by the loading docks and I need y'all to suit back up and get it clean."

"No problem!" Bobby said, and I could see the smirk on his face and knew this was going to be awful.

We suited back up, and I followed Bobby to the other side of the barns. Sure enough, there was a huge pile of liquid shit on the ground outside what looked like a big concrete dock. I moaned, no longer worried about what anyone was thinking of me. We had to go all the way around the building and through more shit to get to where the hoses were.

Bobby handed me a hose and said, "Pull this toward the pile while I unlatch it from back here." Bobby went back to work unwinding the hose and ignoring me, so I did as he'd instructed. I got to the pile just as the hose got caught.

I turned around and jerked it right as I saw Bobby release it. The rest happened in slow motion. I lost my balance and tripped over the oversized waders, falling face-first into the pile of pig shit.

Bobby came rushing up. I could hear the work around me had stopped. When I managed to look up, everyone was looking at me. Several men looked like they were about to laugh. I was beyond done. Some of the shit had even gotten into my mouth. I was spitting when Bobby got to me.

"Oh man, I'm sorry I didn't see you pulling on the hose."

I squared up to him with the most hateful look I could muster and said, "You win, Bobby Devereaux. You didn't have to toss me into a pile of fucking hog shit just to convince me you aren't going to write again."

I was angrier than I think I'd ever been. More than just angry, I was humiliated, fully convinced the asshole had done it on purpose. High school bullies came to mind and I had to resist puking, but not from the hog shit. From humiliation I thought I'd never have to endure again.

"Can someone show me where to go so I can get this shit off of me?" I asked.

Louis rushed over, gave his brother a pointed look, and escorted me to a shower behind the loading dock.

"Can you get my clothes from the living room?" I asked. "I'll change in here."

Louis nodded and rushed away. I was already showering, having washed my body for the tenth time when I heard him come in and put my suit on the rusty radiator outside the shower.

Never mind, I thought. I'll be tossing everything when I get home anyway.

There was no way anyone would be willing to clean the suit after I got back smelling like this.

When I finally felt like I couldn't get any more of the stench off, I got out. Using the clean towel Louis had laid over my suit, I dried off before getting dressed. I came back into the house through the back door. Luckily, all the men had disappeared. When I came in Bobby was sitting in the same place I'd sat before all this began.

"Can you drive me back to my rental now?" I asked.

Bobby stood up and nodded.

"It was an accident, really. I wouldn't push you into shit, no matter how much I don't like you."

I glared at him, then walked out the front door and got into his truck.

When he climbed in, he said, "Not that I don't like you. I was really impressed that you were doing as well as you were."

I stopped him.

"Listen, I'm done. I haven't been this humiliated since I was a kid and bullies took turns punching me in the stomach because the queer boy didn't want to play dodgeball. I can handle most stuff, but humiliation for fun? No. I'm old enough and successful enough, I don't have to deal with that any longer."

The rest of the drive back to Bobby's place was silent. When we got there, I went into his house and picked up my overnight bag. Then, walking past him, I got into my rental and left.

If I never saw the bully again, it'd be too soon.

Bobby Devereaux

I felt like the hog shit Liam had fallen into. He was right, I'd been a bully.

I'd been ashamed of things before. Not being as strong as my brother, not being good enough to play college ball, not being good at math. But I'd never been the guy who caused someone else to feel humiliated. In fact, I'd always been the guy who stood up to the bullies.

I avoided my family for the rest of the day. After cleaning up, I went back to my cold house as punishment. I turned my laptop on and curled up on my bed to stay warm and to deal with my feelings of guilt.

I laid back and the images that came to mind this time were of the bad guy enticing the hero into a cesspool to humiliate him in front of the city.

I made the bad guy ugly and full of himself. I even made it so he took advantage of the hero's natural arrogance.

I wrote for the remainder of the day and into the night. I woke up the next day and kept working, ignoring phone calls and hunger.

The only time I got up was to go to the bathroom or to stretch when my muscles were starting to strain from sitting in one place too long.

On the third day, I got up and ran to my parents' house to grab a quick bite. I ate a leftover biscuit and warmed up coffee, thanking God my parents weren't home, so I didn't have to face them with my way-too-fresh guilt.

I avoided the hog barns and my brother and his men as I jogged back to my place to resume my penitence.

By the next morning, I'd finished the draft.

The story climaxed with the bad guy, intending his cesspool machine to spew vile poison over the entire town, but at the last minute, he changed his mind and sacrificed himself by blowing the machine up before it could blast the city. It was all about showing that my villain had developed a conscience at the last moment, or more precisely, to show Liam how bad I felt about my actions.

I lay down and slept for about eight hours before getting up to shower. When I was clean, I sat at the laptop to review the book and do a few quick edits before I sent it to Roy.

Where the first story had been funny and light-hearted, this one was dark, sad, and reflected the remorse I felt inside for how Liam had ended up during his visit to the farm. It wasn't that I wanted to impress him or make him forgive me. But it did demonstrate, I hoped, how sorry I was that things had turned out the way they had.

In my email to Roy, I wrote,

"I'm sorry for how I treated Mr. Rickard when he came to visit. He was trying to convince me to write a second novel, but I was a total shit to him and that is pretty literal. This is my apology story. I'm not sure if it's publishable, but could you get it to Mr. Rickard anyway? I think if nothing else, he'll get how sorry I am for how I acted."

I sent the email and crawled back under the covers, intending to sleep it off.

The knock on the door a few moments later pulled me out of bed. For some reason, I thought maybe it was Liam, and I opened the door fully prepared to apologize. Instead, my HVAC guy stood looking at me with a giant smile.

"I bet you're happy to see me," he said.

I smiled back, indeed happy to see him. The furnace had to be completely replaced, which took the guy all day. I ended up having to help him since his son, who usually worked with him, couldn't be there because he'd just lost his mom, the HVAC guy's ex-wife.

By dinnertime, I had heat. Feeling the warm air flowing through the old ductwork made me happy. The HVAC guy promised he'd be back when his son was on the job, so they could replace the old ductwork.

I decided it was time to go eat crow at home. Bringing my laptop along, I followed the HVAC guy out and drove to my parents' house.

Everyone was sitting at the table, somehow knowing I was ready to come clean about my behavior.

I sat down and said, "Okay, I was a total shit and I fucked up." My mom gave me *the look* and I shrugged. "Okay, I screwed up, then."

"How's he doing?" Louis asked.

I shrugged. "Not sure. Last I heard he was telling me I was a bully. Which, of course, was spot on."

"Whatcha gonna do?" Dad asked.

I just shook my head.

"I already did it. He came here for a story and I wrote him one. But this time, the hero and the villain looked an awful lot alike."

My dad smiled and patted my shoulder.

"That's usually the reality of it, isn't it? We're all the bad guy sometimes."

I nodded.

"Well, anyway, I have the first draft here if anyone wants to read it. Mostly it's me apologizing through fiction."

Both my siblings exclaimed at the same time, "I wanna read it!"

Everyone at the table laughed. There's no one like your brother and sister to keep it real.

Liam Rickard

I had avoided opening the email from Roy. I didn't really want to see what Bobby Devereaux had sent, although I knew if he'd written another book, my pride needed to get out of the way so I could get it worked up and published before the next New York Comic-Con.

I called Irene in. "Get me a martini, maybe two."

"No, it's too early," she said and walked out of my office. Sometimes I hated her, but mostly I didn't. She came back a few moments later with a mimosa.

"This is an appropriate breakfast drink," she said with a wink and left my office.

I shook my head as I downed the drink and hollered for Irene to make me another one. I knew she wouldn't, but at least it felt good to pretend like I was in charge.

I opened the document and read.

By the fifth chapter, I was crying. There was no laughter in this book. Instead, remorse poured out in one of the most eloquent ways I've ever seen. The man was a master of his craft even if he was arrogant and flat-out bull-headed.

Unlike the first novel, this one was dark and foreboding. If it hadn't been for the first book's main character, you wouldn't have been able to tell it was even written by the same man. Both pieces were brilliant. My only concern was that this one was such a complete shift from the first novel, I wasn't sure if it would work with his previous demographic.

I sent it back to Roy and told him to work up the edits and see if Devereaux—I couldn't get myself to call him Bobby—would be willing to work them out.

Roy got back to me a half-hour later and told me Bobby was on board and they were starting right away.

I leaned back, feeling just a little guilty. Yes, I'd been humiliated, but the guy was obviously remorseful. It was clear that was the only reason he'd written the damned thing. It felt a lot like manipulation to publish a piece I knew he'd resisted writing so much.

I called Doug and told him to meet me in my office to discuss Devereaux's new book.

"What new book?" he asked.

He didn't know. That wasn't a good sign.

"I'll send it over," I said. "Roy is working out the edits now."

"You guys do this backward, you know," Doug huffed. "The agent is supposed to get the manuscript and send it to the publisher!"

"I know that, Doug. I didn't know he was going to be sending it, but I know why he did. You'll see when you read it. It's...different."

Doug sighed.

"Push the meeting to tomorrow morning. I'm going to read the whole thing. I need to know what I'm dealing with."

I transferred him over to Irene, who set up the appointment. It was strange. Roy, Doug, and Devereaux were the only people I had this bizarre relationship with. I maintained a strict chain of command with everyone else, and no other agent would bite my head off for not following protocol. But everything about Bobby Devereaux caused confusion and warped the reality around him.

Even if I had believed he meant to humiliate me before, I definitely didn't think so now. I needed to have a heart-to-heart with Doug about the ethics of publishing a novel that was written out of guilt.

Bobby was right, people thought I was a monster. I knew I was tough to work with, but I did have some fucking scruples, and even if I wanted the book, I wasn't willing to ignore his wishes to get it.

The next morning, Doug sat across from me sipping the latte Irene had prepared for him.

"It's gut-wrenching," he said. "What did you do to pull this out of him?"

"Let's just say, all it took was a heavy dose of humiliation."

When Doug looked at me askance, I added, "My humiliation. I went to visit him in Iowa, and he wasn't happy I showed up. In fact, I pissed him off quite a bit. To be honest, looking back, it was more than a little arrogant of me to show up unannounced and expect to stay at his place. I agreed to help him on his parents' farm—which is a total nightmare, just so you know—and ended up face-down in a pile of liquid hog shit."

I chuckled to myself. "I may be the only person to fly first-class, wearing Armani and smelling like a hog barn, but that's basically how it all came down. Anyway, I was home a week, thinking we'd seen the last of your client when the email came with the manuscript attached. Doug, here's my dilemma. He was clear to you, Roy, and even me that he wasn't writing again. If I hadn't ended up calling him a bully and making him feel guilty, I doubt he'd have written this one. I have no doubt from notoriety alone, this would be a successful novel. When you add in the quality of it, I think we'll bring in a whole different set of Devereaux fans with this one. It's possibly worth millions. So, you see my dilemma."

Doug looked at me oddly.

"You know you're the only publisher in the country who'd think about this twice. The rest of them would all jump on it and not give a crap what Devereaux thinks. At least, not after he sent the draft to them."

"Well, he still has to sign a contract. And I don't think this is the last we're going to see of him, no matter what he says. I'd prefer not to lose him to a competitor."

Doug nodded. "He has an innate talent. I suspect he'll write again, but I wonder if he's in the wrong genre."

I shrugged. "I'll let you and him figure that out. But for now, I need you to have this discussion before we negotiate any contracts. He and Roy are already working through edits." When Doug shot me a look, I put my hands up. "I know, I know, but when has anything been done by the book where Devereaux is concerned?"

Doug finished off his latte, stood up, and shrugged. "Never, but that's what makes him special, I think."

I nodded and we shook hands as he left my office.

I had a trip planned to London the next day. I was more than a bit happy to have a distraction from all this. I wanted that manuscript so much I could taste it, but I didn't want to be the arrogant asshole Devereaux thought I was.

And why? I asked myself that repeatedly. I didn't know why. Because he was different? Because he could see through me in a way no one else, including my family, could? Because he wasn't afraid of me but wasn't an asshole either?

I began trying to shut him out of my mind, knowing my obsessive personality could persevere on this subject for hours to come.

I put loud rock music on and began packing my suitcases. Nothing was able to fully get the man out of my head, though, and I ended up lying on my bed staring at the ceiling for hours before I fell asleep, my head full of thoughts about the talented Bobby Devereaux.

Bobby Devereaux

I laughed when Doug told me Liam was concerned about accepting the contract, feeling guilty about why I'd written the book.

"If I didn't want him to publish it, I wouldn't have sent it to him, Doug."

"I know, but apparently, he's concerned. So he wanted me to make sure you were committed to it before he offered a contract."

"Well, we need to talk about the contract," I said. "Like last time, I won't be committing to writing another book. Also, I'm not running all over the fucking world signing books again. I'm willing to do the Comic-Cons because those are fun and just the right amount of geeky, but besides those, I'll only do four other book signings."

"You know that's not gonna fly," Doug warned.

"Well, it's gonna fly if they want to publish. I hate the book signings and the readings and all that. It's just not who I am. I can live through a few of them, but four is my limit."

"You're a spoiled brat, Bobby Devereaux. I'm sure you're gonna get away with this, but you have to know you're the only one who does."

I laughed.

"I'm not spoiled, Doug. I just have good boundaries."

"You'd be poor with good boundaries if your last novel hadn't sold so well."

"On a different subject, do you think we can get Riedell Lewis to do the graphic art again? I think we should put this one out as a graphic novel from the very beginning. I sell two hundred graphic novels to every book and make the same amount of money per sale either way."

"I can't see why not. I'll talk to them about getting that all put into the contract when we write it up."

"Thanks, Doug. You're the best!"

"Yeah, yeah. I'll talk to you soon."

It took a lot longer to get the contracts back than I'd thought it would. I was thinking they were going to reject it when I finally got the email from Doug, basically giving me everything I'd asked for.

Work on the graphic novel was to begin immediately, which I was strangely excited about.

I wasn't someone who could draw. Seriously, I'd never even considered being a novelist who wrote comic books. But I really liked Riedell. She was smart, witty, and illustrated her own graphic novels as well.

When I described a character to her, the way I saw them in my head, she drew them perfectly, like she could see inside my mind. That fascinated me, and even when I hadn't been planning to write again, she and I had emailed and texted back and forth.

When we'd worked on the first book, we'd done so over the phone using some fancy software the publisher had sent us. I demanded that we be able to work in person on the second graphic novel, mostly because I wanted to get to know her better.

That was a good call because as I sat in her large open-air studio apartment in the middle of Saratoga Springs, New York, we spent as much time laughing and enjoying each other as we did working. The result was I now had a great new friend, and the graphic novel was at least fifty percent better than the previous one.

The movie version of *Vortex Prism was released in November.* In the midst of helping edit and fix my graphic novel, I was wined and dined by Hollywood and had even been invited to meet all the actors and see them shooting. It was fun, of course. But, like my time living with my ex, all the hoopla and pretense just went over my head.

My family were all flying out with me for the première, and the movie studio had said we didn't need to worry about clothes. We just needed to get to the studio a few hours early and they'd dress us and pretty us up.

I made my brother stay out of the hog barns for a week so he wouldn't smell like ammonia, which he teased me about mercilessly.

"Don't want a hick farmer stinking up your fancy theater?" he asked.

"Um, do you want to be sitting next to Hollywood's A-List smelling like hog shit?" I asked him, and his smile faded.

"Which A-List will I be sitting next to?"

When I told him, his face paled.

"I'm a hog farmer. I can't sit next to them."

Mom walked in as he said that and pointed her finger at him.

"I'll not have any of that talk, young man," she said. "You are every bit as good as them, and I bet every one of them enjoys the bacon that's served in their fancy restaurants. That wouldn't be happening if it wasn't for us."

I didn't dare tell her they were all mostly vegan.

Regardless, Louis' face lit up with pride. I didn't know my brother could be starstruck and I wondered why I never was.

The première night came, and we arrived at the theater. I was so pleased my family looked right at home with the Hollywood crowd. Both my sister and brother looked amazing on the red carpet. Paparazzi snapped pictures of them both like they were big stars, and they smiled and posed like they were. Thanks to my mom's Latin background and my dad's French and Swiss roots, we weren't a bad-looking bunch. Hog farmers we were, but I was proud my family stood toe-to-toe with the pretty Hollywood crowd.

Liam was at the première as well. I wanted to tell him how much I hated what happened, but we weren't able to talk much.

Mom and Louis both greeted him, and we were all a bit awkward since this was the first time we'd seen each other since the unfortunate hog shit incident.

Liam sat with the movie's producer on the other side of the theater. He looked at me as I walked past him to go to our seats. My heart began to beat faster upon seeing him. I couldn't tell what his expression said. Was there animosity? Maybe. The man was all business as he sat there with his tailored suit that fit his body perfectly. I sighed with regret as I walked toward my seat and my family.

Liam was an attractive and savvy businessman, and I knew he was the reason this movie was happening. I'd been annoyed that night when he came into my home all cocky and arrogant, but under different circumstances, I could've probably learned to like him. He was, unfortunately, my type in every way. Tall, brooding, handsome and yes, even arrogant.

The movie was great, both funny and light-hearted like I'd written the novel to be. I laughed more than others did, knowing the underlying meaning of much of the plot. Poor Randy would be mortified if he knew this was based on him. I almost felt guilty about it, but not too much, he really was an asshole.

The *Des Moines Register* posted pictures of our family looking elegant on the front page, and for a few weeks we were the stars of our little town. Then we all got back to work, and stardom faded into the humdrum of living life on a farm.

By New Years', the graphics and writing for the project were done and the book had gone through the editing process. Rickard Publishing had announced my next book was coming out.

Doug had done a couple interviews since I'd flatly refused to. He announced this graphic novel was vastly different, darker, more morose, and carrying a different message. I could tell they were preparing the audience for the new direction this book had taken.

The release was due the same week as New York Comic-Con, just like the previous one. Comic-Con New York happens in February, which was only a couple months away. Unlike the first novel, the publisher was doing a lot more to promote the book this time.

By the time February came around, almost five months had passed since the unfortunate poop incident. I was ready to get the second book out into the world. There was something about this graphic novel that was different for me. It was more genuine and looked at the real issues of how easy it is to slip into the role of the villain, even when we don't think we're being bad people.

To my dismay, I was asked to spend time in New York to discuss strategy and to finalize my four agreed-upon tour duties as well as the other Comic-Cons I would attend after the novel was released. Oh well, the fact that this new contract allowed me to be free ninety percent of the time made it worth the ten percent I wasn't too fond of.

I got off the plane, feeling a little guilty about sitting in first class while so many others were crammed together like sardines. I honestly thought the whole differential treatment based on class was stupid. If they removed first class and used that extra space to give everyone more legroom, they'd make the same amount of money, and everyone would be happier.

I grabbed my luggage, walked toward the exits where I'd been told to meet my driver, and came face-to-face with Liam Rickard.

I stopped in my tracks, surprised that my initial reaction was to turn and go the other way. Something about this man messed with my insides. I couldn't quite tell if I was repulsed, angry, or infatuated with him. I shook all that off as he watched me with those intense eyes of his. I forced myself to smile.

"Hi, Liam. This is an honor."

He laughed. "You're a bad liar."

"Whatever. I *should* be honored."

He lifted an eyebrow the way he'd done on the farm when he was amused or annoyed.

He let the *should* part go and escorted me to the car waiting in the valet area of the airport. I didn't realize there was a valet at the airport.

Learn new things every day. I thought to myself, rolling my eyes.

I tried to be cynical over the Bentley Mulsanne as the valet pulled it around the drive and toward us, but that's where my geekiness kicked up a notch. I loved cars. I didn't really know much about them, but I knew beauty. And Bentleys were still masterpieces of art and style.

I schooled my face, not wanting to let Liam know I liked it, but I could tell by his expression that Liam had seen my pleasure. After he got into his seat, I sat in the back, treating him like my driver, just to give him a jolt.

I was intentionally trying to harass him, just to get past his perfect businessman demeanor, but unfortunately, when I looked in the mirror and saw his face, he was smiling.

As we drove toward the office, he peppered me with questions about how things were at home.

"How's your brother?"

"He's fine, thanks."

"Did your family enjoy the première?"

"Yes, they were surprised how much they liked it."

I answered several more questions before I finally sighed and said, "Liam, I'm really sorry about what happened, I didn't..."

He held up his hand.

"Apology accepted. And thank you for stepping up to the plate with that last novel. It's wonderful and was a better apology than anything you were going to say. Let's put all that behind us."

I chuckled.

"Arrogant," I said, making him smile again.

When we got to the office and parked in his reserved spot, I was in a good mood. I knew Liam was the CEO and the truth was he held my life in his hands, at least to a point. But I liked teasing him, and the fact that he handled it well gave him major coolness points.

I followed him up to his office and we sat at an opulent round table. His assistant, Irene, was already there.

She brought us both coffee without asking if we wanted it. My flight had been ridiculously early in the morning and the airport coffee had been less than appealing. I tended to be either a total, all-out coffee snob, or I just wanted my mom's drip coffee. Nothing in between seemed to work for me.

Luckily, this latte was top of the line. When I thanked Irene, telling her how much I liked it, she winked at me.

When Liam laid out my new schedule, pointing out the four book signings I'd be doing, I couldn't help but smile.

"You're sending me to London, Tokyo, Berlin, and Rio de Janeiro?" I asked, surprised.

"Yep," he said.

I shook my head. "That's weird. Why are they all out of the country?"

"Because your first book's sales are really beginning to take off in those cities. Besides, you've already committed to the Comic-Cons here in the States."

I nodded. "Well, I'm not going to complain if that's what you think is best."

His smile showed his pleasure. "I didn't think you would, but you never know. You authors are a tough breed to read."

"Hmm," I said, leaning back in the chair. "So that's it? You called me a week early to come to your office and agree to this?"

I heard Irene snicker in the background, causing her boss to give her a nasty look.

"Well, if you were going to be difficult, I needed enough time to persuade you."

"I guess in that case, I could drive up and visit Riedell."

The guy's face actually fell.

Aha! I figured there was more going on, I thought.

I waited to see how he was going to manage this.

"You could, or you could stay and go to dinner with me tonight, so I can show you off to New York's elite."

I acted like I was gagging. "No, thank you. That sounds awful. Unless it would help with the book release, which I seriously doubt since the New York elite wouldn't waste their time on my book. To be honest, I'd rather eat dirt."

Irene coughed and you could tell she was trying not to laugh. Liam told her to check with Roy to see if he was prepared for the meeting they had coming up.

She smirked as she walked by and said, "I like this one, Captain."

I think I like her too. I thought to myself.

"So, what would you like to do then?" he asked me.

I leaned back in my chair.

"Well, if you're willing to trust me," I said, thinking mischievously. "I've got a couple of ideas."

He studied me for a moment. "I'm not sure I do trust you, but as long as you can promise nothing will involve manure, I'm open."

"What's your day like now?" I asked.

He looked over to where Irene had been sitting and, remembering she was gone, got up and went to her desk.

"I have several things to do this morning, but I could move the afternoon stuff around."

I smiled. "Then I have a couple places I'd like to see while I'm here. It's possible you might like them too."

He nodded. "It's a date," he said before backtracking. "It's a *professional* date."

I laughed. "If you think I'm sexy, you don't have to pretend," I said, just as Irene walked in.

She almost lost it in the doorway.

Liam's face was bright red. If I hadn't still felt a little guilty about the shit bath he'd taken at my family's farm, I'd have burst out laughing.

"Let's keep it professional," Liam said, standing.

"I'll see you at noon then?" I asked. "Shall I meet you here?"

He nodded and I turned to leave.

"Oh, if you have something a little less formal, you might want to put that on," I said and slipped out the office door before he could respond.

Liam Rickard

The man unsettled me. I'd invited him to come to New York early with every intention of wining and dining him, letting him know we were okay, good even. Instead, he took over and turned my plans on a dime.

I should've known better. When I thought about it, the first book had been all about the ridiculousness of the overindulgent. I wouldn't be impressing him with expensive dinners and big names.

I kept thinking about what I was in for as the morning meetings dragged on and on. Finally, when we broke for lunch, I went back to my office and changed into the jeans and t-shirt I'd worn the last time I was working through the weekend. I'd meant to take them home to wash at the very least, but it hadn't happened. It was lucky for me, as it turned out since I could now accommodate Bobby's request.

New York was cold in February but we'd had an unseasonably warm front move in. So, I figured I'd get away with just my leather jacket.

I had just come out of my office when Bobby walked in. I had the pleasure of seeing his face as he caught sight of me. His eyes dropped to examine my outfit. I swallowed hard at his expression and felt my cock stir. I'll admit I was attracted to Bobby, and if I'm honest, that's probably why I invited him early, but damn...I hadn't expected to see the look of pure lust on his face, at least not without some wooing on my part.

I shook it off and looked at Irene, who was grinning from ear to ear. That woman was too much.

"Irene, we'll be back..."

I looked at Bobby again and he cleared his throat.

"Yeah..." he said while shaking his head. "We won't be back today."

He grinned at Irene and she winked at him. It was the second time today she'd done that. It was unnerving because the woman didn't usually wink at people.

"Okay, then. Text or call if you need me," I said as we walked out the door.

I stepped toward the garage elevator and Bobby took my arm.

"We should take the subway," he said and with his arm in mine, he pushed the button that would take us down to the first floor.

I let him lead me through the busy streets and down into the bowels of the city. It wasn't like I hadn't ridden the subway before. I rode it when I knew I was going to be drinking. Okay, no, that wasn't true, I usually used a taxi, but I had used the subway a lot when I was younger.

We bought our tickets, and next thing I knew, we were packed into the subway car speeding toward God only knew where.

We had to get off and change cars three times before Bobby finally pulled me off at Canal Street. It had been a long time since I'd been down here. My best friend in high school had relatives in Little Italy, so I knew where we were, but it wasn't a place I frequented. We walked a few blocks until we were on Mulberry Street.

"You hungry?" he asked.

I nodded as my stomach growled. I hadn't eaten anything yet, having forgone breakfast in favor of picking him up at the airport.

We turned several corners until he finally escorted me into a total dive of a place. I looked around and although it appeared to be clean enough, the place looked like it hadn't been renovated since 1976. It took everything in me not to curl my nose up, but Bobby was watching me, and knowing he had probably predicted that response, I held my expression.

"You like pizza, pasta, or are you open to surprises?" he asked.

I shrugged. "Anything but snails."

He smiled. "I'll have two calzones, Benny's special. Just try not to make it too spicy this time," he said to the clerk at the counter.

He sat me down at a seat by the window. Then he walked over to the part of the restaurant where there were groceries and wines for sale. I watched him, fascinated with this strange little shop and restaurant combination, as he took a bottle of wine to the front desk, bought it, and asked the woman to open it and bring us some glasses.

She followed him to the table, and he sat down and poured us each a glass. A few minutes later, the lady came back with a basket of bread, along with a couple of plates. Bobby poured some olive oil and balsamic vinegar onto his plate, and pulling a piece of the bread off, dipped it in the savory combination.

He popped it into his mouth and moaned.

"Oh!" he said, his mouth still full. "I've missed this."

I didn't respond but watched him, imagining for a moment what it would feel like to reach over and kiss the oil off his lips. He took a sip of wine and moaned again.

This time, the moan did funny things to my insides. More to steady myself than anything else, I took a sip of the wine. My eyes must have looked like saucers. It was like I was drinking some of my dad's most expensive wine from his collection.

"What the hell, this is delicious. Did you just drop a grand on this or something?" I asked.

Bobby shook his head. "Try $29.95."

"Get out of here!" I said, turning the wine around until I could see the label. Clearly it was imported, but not one I'd heard of before. This one was from Portugal and it had a perfect body and texture. How were they selling this for thirty bucks?

Bobby continued eating bread dipped in the vinegar mix, so I grabbed a piece of bread and dipped it into his mixture.

"Hey, get your own," he chastised me.

I tossed the bread into my mouth and, ignoring his admonishment, dipped another piece.

"This is good," I said.

"Wait till you taste the calzone. They're different every time as long as you say you want Benny's special. That's just whatever they have lying around, I think."

I looked at him skeptically, but he just smiled. "You're so pretentious. Trust me, you're gonna love it."

I shrugged. Taking another sip of my wine and smirking, I said, "Pretentious..."

But I knew he was right. I wouldn't be caught dead in a place like this usually, and I didn't really eat calzones. I sometimes had a pizza if a Michelin Star chef was experimenting, but seldom a regular pizza.

The same woman who served us before brought our calzones to the table. They were still steaming hot. Bobby cut his in half, opened it, and let the steam roll out. He let it rest there while he continued eating bread and sipping wine.

I did the same, figuring he knew what he was doing.

"So, the new book is exciting. We did a panel with the same group who reviewed your first book and they loved it. I'm guessing it'll be as popular as your first and hopefully even more so."

Bobby smiled but didn't really respond other than to say he hoped so.

"I've never been to Rio de Janeiro or to Tokyo," he admitted. "I'm excited to see them."

"You've been to Europe then?" I asked.

Bobby broke out into a guarded smile. "Yeah, but it was with the family. London was a total disaster."

"Really? Why?" I asked.

"Let's just say we had a bit of a culture shock and my brother and sister didn't manage that so well."

I laughed, wanting to get more out of him but he changed the subject. "Berlin was more fun for all of us, though. We were only there for a couple days, so there wasn't as much time for my brother to get bored or my sister to poke at him."

I asked him what he meant by his sister poking his brother and he laughed. Before responding, he cut off a section of the calzone and put it into his mouth. The wine and bread moan had stirred something in me, but watching him eat the calzone, seeing the cheese land next to his perfectly shaped mouth and watching his expression—which had to be the same expression he made when he came—caused all the blood in my head to drain into my quickly hardening cock.

When he looked at me, his expression went from happy to shock and then to lustful. He swallowed the calzone, making me think of the look he'd given me when he saw me in my jeans and t-shirt. The conversation about his family in Europe was forgotten.

For lack of anything else to do, I took a bite of the calzone. My own moan slipped through my lips.

"This is fantastic," I said. "I can see why you love it so much."

His lustful expression shifted to happiness. "See, it doesn't have to be a fancy meal to be good."

I smiled and took another drink. "You think I only eat fancy meals?" I asked.

He gave me an all-knowing look and asked, "Do you eat anything that isn't fancy?"

"Yeah," I lied.

He'd already figured me out, though, and just smiled, not contradicting me.

The banter between us was light and fun. He really was enjoyable to be around. For the most part he wasn't judgmental, although I think he had me pretty well pegged. In any other situation, with any other person, I wouldn't have minded at all. But under his beautiful gaze, I felt like I was lacking.

After we'd eaten as much as we could—neither of us had finished the second half of our respective calzones—he asked the woman at the counter to put both of the remains into different doggie bags.

As she bagged our calzones, he poured the rest of the wine into my glass after topping his off and lifted his glass.

"Here's to book two, and a faceplant into shit." When I gave him the eye, he shrugged. "Bad as it was, there would be no book two if that hadn't happened."

I lifted my glass and hesitantly clinked it with his.

He finished his wine in one huge gulp. When he stood to take the doggie bag from the lady, I was forced to do the same.

As we walked down Mulberry Street, he wrapped his arm around mine, similar to the way he'd done when he led me away from the garage elevator that morning. It was unclear if it was to stave off the cool breeze or to just be close, but I liked it, whatever his reasoning.

We walked until we came to a couple of old homeless men sitting on Hester. He took my bag, rushed over to them, and handed them the bags of food.

"Al, Dave," he said.

"Whoa, if it isn't the little lost sheep," one of the old guys said. He had a heavy accent that sounded like it belonged in Brooklyn more than Manhattan.

"Went home for a spell," Bobby said. And when the two men stood up, he shook their hands and gave them each a hug.

"You two eat well. This is Benny's special."

"Oh, those taste so good," the other man said as his friend nodded.

"Don't eat it all at once, you know how you have stomach issues, Dave."

"Yeah, yeah... get lost, kid!"

Bobby laughed heartily and waved goodbye as he came back over to me.

"Who are they?" I asked.

He looked back fondly at the two homeless men and said, "Uncle Dave and Uncle Al."

"Your uncles live on the streets of Manhattan?" I asked, confused.

Bobby's entire face broke out into a smile as he linked his arm through mine again.

"You're so gullible. No, they're a couple guys I knew from when I lived here. They're a gay couple, been together like a million years."

"Why are they homeless?" I asked.

Bobby looked sad and pulled his arm away from mine. The feeling of losing his closeness made me want to weep.

"Why is anyone homeless?" he asked. "For a lot of gay people, life still isn't easy. Homelessness still impacts gay people disproportionately, but I really never asked. Regardless, they are two of my favorite people from my life in the city."

I didn't respond, the guy was an oddball. He had no interest in a high-end meal, preferring a calzone at Benny's or whatever the restaurant was called. His best buddies while living in New York were a homeless gay couple. What was I dealing with here?

We continued to walk until we got to Canal and turning right, we walked in silence until we got to Lafayette.

"Are you planning to kill me or something?" I asked when we turned down the odd street.

"Hah!" he said. "No, I could've done that at the hog barn if I'd wanted to. Or let you freeze in my house last year. I'm taking you to my favorite museum."

I looked at him strangely since we'd just walked past New York City's Rescue Mission.

"A museum here?"

He smiled. "You'll see."

We walked to the middle of the block. Sitting there was a bizarre-looking open area with the word *Mmuseumm* printed next to it.

"They misspelled the word," I said.

"I think that's the point," Bobby responded as he walked around me.

I almost remarked, duh, but was caught by the odd display in front of me.

It was located in a freight elevator and there were random things on the shelves. A glove, a piece of tape, a pair of underwear, and several other equally bizarre items.

Bobby watched me as I looked around and read the descriptions, completely confused about what I was looking at. He wandered around behind me, looking at each of them. Occasionally he'd smile or scratch his head.

I didn't have a clue what any of this was about. Random stuff put on shelves made no sense to me.

I finally gave up trying to figure it out and just enjoyed watching him. If I hadn't already been completely perplexed, I would've been for sure as he went from item to item looking at the display like he was looking at a Rembrandt or Van Gogh.

When we finally walked out, I looked at him questioningly and he shrugged.

"Object Journalism," he said, like that made everything clear.

"That's the strangest thing I've ever seen in my life," I said.

"That's 'cause you don't have a soul," he replied. "Don't worry, I can help you find one."

I just shook my head. This guy was too much.

We wandered through Chinatown, shopping for nothing, chatting about nonsense, and generally enjoying each other's company.

Bobby was affectionate and he had no inhibitions about touching me in public. The touches weren't even sexual, at least not yet. But the looks we kept giving each other all day indicated that was likely to change. He touched my hand when he wanted to draw my attention to something or pulled himself into my side when we were just walking.

The effect was that he'd completely inserted me into his life and showed me his perspective, which was about as opposite from my own as any could be.

We took the subway back to the office.

When we got back, he said, "Want me to just grab a taxi or do you want to take me to my hotel?"

Duh! I thought to myself. Like I was going to let him go that quickly, not after a day of virtual edging.

"I'll take you," I said.

He shot me a knowing smile as we rode the elevator to the level where my car was parked. He climbed in after me and laid his hand over mine as I put the car into reverse.

"I'd like for you to come up with me to my room," he said.

I didn't respond. Instead, I thought about how he'd controlled the entire day. It was just like how he'd controlled the time I'd been at his home. I wasn't used to letting others be in control, and, unfortunately, I let that dictate my response.

When I pulled up in front of the Hilton, I said, "I don't think that's a good idea."

His face fell and I felt my heart break for disappointing him, all the more reason not to get too involved. With resolve I didn't have, I got his bags out of the back of the Bentley, handed them to the bellhop, and said I'd see him the next day.

As I pulled out of the drop-off lane, I saw him watching me leave. I knew deep down that I'd royally screwed this one up.

Bobby Devereaux

I watched him pull away and felt the raw sting of rejection. Something I hadn't felt since I chased a football player in college who wasn't that into me. The bellhop tapped me on the shoulder, and I followed him into the hotel to check-in.

As you'd expect, the hotel was beautiful. The rooms were nice yet understated. I knew Liam had dropped a pretty penny for me to stay here. Even though I was about as uninterested in pretension as you could get, I'd seen some of New York's alternatives and I strongly preferred this to them.

I took a long soak in the big tub, using some of the fancy soaps which made my skin feel smooth and made me happy. By the time I got out and rinsed off all the bubbles in the shower, I had resolved to let things go with Liam Rickard.

One, he was a pretentious, aristocratic New York snob, the type I had sworn I'd never get involved with again. And two, he was the CEO of the publishing house that currently had control over my books. With little to no effort, they could make my life difficult. I had no business chasing this man. Which meant I had absolutely no common sense, considering I'd thrown myself at him all damned day.

I pushed away the fact that he smelled good and that he looked like James Dean in that tight t-shirt and those designer jeans. Oh, and when he put the leather jacket on, I almost creamed myself. None of that mattered because we had nothing in common. Not only was I a country boy from the sticks of Iowa, but I was damned proud to be one.

Where Liam thrived on overpriced, tiny plates of food, I liked a steak, or ribs, or a huge Sunday barbeque, or all of those choices at the same time.

The only thing pretentious about me was that I loved Broadway and even the opera. However, I had liked those back when I was growing up in Iowa, before I'd ever gotten to New York. Besides, I think I liked both of those as much for the grit it took to produce them as I did the big, over-the-top productions themselves.

I tossed myself onto the gloriously comfortable bed, then crawled off and peeled the covers back to get a look at the brand of the mattress.

"I will totally be buying one of these for my place," I said out loud as I snapped a picture of the label with my phone.

After putting the bed back together, I plopped down and felt sorry for myself.

"Why do I always fall for the stupid rich guys who don't have a clue or a personality?" I asked the room.

Because you secretly like people who are your opposite. I heard the voice inside my brain say.

I purposefully ignored the voice and turned over on my side. Luckily, before the voice could start a big discussion about my idiosyncrasies, I fell into blissful sleep. The only thing that disturbed me was the fact that I dreamed of Liam's beautiful hands gently caressing my body.

I woke up early the next morning, mostly because I'd fallen asleep too early. I threw on my workout clothes and went to the hotel's gym. I wasn't the only one there, but luckily this hotel had more options than just a treadmill. I worked out, more to keep up my stamina than to get buff after spending so much time doing manual labor on the pig farm.

I'd learned quickly after moving back home that I did better when I got some exercise. If I let my body get slack, I tended to get depressed and moody. With the book release coming up, I wanted...no, if I were going to change my plans for the future and truly see myself writing like this full time, as a career, I *needed* to keep my mind sharp.

By the time I got back to my room, I felt like a man with a mission. I ordered a latte to be delivered. When in Rome, act like a Roman, right? Then I took a shower.

I dressed and, after drinking my latte, I took the subway to go shopping. I didn't have the right clothes for Comic-Con. It'd been so long since I'd been shopping that I decided I'd splurge on this trip and get a few outfits I could use for the events.

New York is ridiculously expensive. People always think once your books hit it big, and especially when you get a movie deal, you're all kinds of rich. Too bad that isn't true. I sighed inwardly, knowing I should've found something more reasonable in Des Moines, but if I was going to play in a world that gave a shit about this kind of stuff, I needed to play the part.

There were several designer places that carried clothes I would feel more comfortable wearing than suits. I thought of Liam in his Armani and although he was sexy, the suits did nothing for him compared to the designer t-shirt and jeans he'd worn yesterday.

That was the image I had in my mind as I browsed the Manhattan shops.

After a massive, over-the-top dent to my credit cards, I had bag after bag delivered to my hotel room. I forced myself not to think about all the food this money could've bought for people like Al and Dave.

Unable to get it out of my head, I used my phone to sign onto the New York Rescue Mission website and donated about ten percent of what I'd just spent to the mission. Although my salary as a journalist had often barely covered my expenses, the mission had been one of the few places I consistently donated to while living in the city. The donation didn't make what I'd just spent any better or justify it in any way, but at least if I was going to throw money around like an idiot, they could benefit some as well.

The bags were all waiting for me in my room when I arrived, and I began unpacking them and sticking their contents in drawers. Believe it or not, I could've elected for the hotel to do it for me, at an extra cost, of course. I considered it for a moment since the hotel costs were being billed directly to Liam's company. Instead, I shook off the thought. I was only being vindictive because Liam had rejected my advances...and I was a better person than that. At least, I was working on being a better person than that.

I looked at my phone for the first time since I'd made my donation and noticed I had three texts from Doug asking where I was.

I texted him back, saying I was getting ready for Comic-Con and doing some shopping.

A few moments later he responded.

Liam's looking for you.

I rolled my eyes.

He doesn't need anything. We got it all handled yesterday in like a two-minute meeting. Tell him to buzz off!

I got a text back with three question marks.

It's nothing, we hung out together yesterday. If he needed anything for the book, I'm sure he'd have asked me then.

Doug called two seconds after he got the message and I answered. "What do you mean you and he spent the day together yesterday?"

"Just that I took him up to my favorite part of the city and we hung out."

"And..."

"And what?" I asked.

"You know damned well what. I'm your agent Bobby, you need to keep me informed of this stuff."

"Why weren't you there for yesterday's meeting?" I asked.

"I wasn't invited, or I would've been," Doug replied.

"Well, when you find out what he wants to meet about, let me know."

Doug called back about an hour later, laughing his ass off.

"So, I get the impression your meeting yesterday was less about the book and more about...something else," he said.

"I can't see why you'd think that."

Even though I knew I had all but thrown myself at Liam, and he had driven away, saying coming up to my hotel room would be a bad idea. It had been a bad idea, of course, but still...

"Well, when I talked to Irene, she said he turned a shade of purple when you wanted to know what the meeting was about."

Good. I thought.

"Did you find out the reason for the meeting?"

"No, she said she'd get back to me about the agenda."

"Well, in that case, why don't I just go on with my day, you go on with yours, and we'll see if he comes up with something?"

"You're cruel," Doug replied.

"No, I'm not. The dude needs to learn that he can't always get his way just because he waves his hand. I flew out here a whole week early and then it takes a few minutes to do what I flew here for. If he has another agenda, he needs to spit it out, 'cause I've lost all patience."

Doug sighed. "I think you're playing a dangerous game here. If he wanted to, he could pull the plug and leave you in the dirt, Bobby."

I laughed. "Remember, I only wrote the book to apologize to him for being an ass. If he wants to pull the plug, he can pull it. Meanwhile, we may want to start looking at other publishers in case I decide to write again."

"That's not so easy, at least for this series. They pretty much have first right of refusal for any other books written."

"But not for new characters and storylines. I know. My attorneys looked over the contract before I signed it. I'm not a total idiot, Doug."

"Still, I wouldn't jump the gun just yet. If things get tough between you two, then we'll talk. Until then, I recommend you not do anything to piss the boss off."

I hmphed at that. "He ain't my boss."

Doug hesitated. "Just walk lightly. I know you're an independent spirit, but Liam is a powerful man and used to getting his way. We've all pushed the boundaries with him, but it's still unwise to push too far."

After hanging up, I thought about what he said. The more I did, the more upset I became. Before I knew it, I was headed out the door wearing the designer t-shirt and pants I'd just purchased, not thinking about the tags still being on.

When I got to the top floor of the building where Liam's office was, Irene was just coming out of his office.

"Is he available?" I asked.

She smiled and nodded. "Just go on in."

Before I lost my nerve, I went in and plopped down in the chair across from a surprised Liam.

"Listen, I know you're busy, so I won't stay long, but I have questions that need to be answered. Are you interested in me? I mean *really interested*, like for more than just someone you can get to write books for you?"

He stared at me. I swear he was giving me the same look he had the day before, which was why I thought maybe he wanted me for more than...well, for more than writing books.

When he didn't respond, I got up and started pacing.

"Okay, well, that says a lot right there. I guess I got my wires crossed and thought you might want more. Now my agent is telling me to walk on fucking eggshells and not to piss you off, so you don't crush my book or something. So, here's the deal. If you wanna control me, Mr. Rickard, then you need to give that shit up 'cause I'm not someone to control or manipulate. I'm my own man and all I owe you, or really, all I owe your company, is what we have contracted." I was beginning to feel my juices flowing. "I offer you respect, and when I fuck up, I apologize like a respectable person. But you aren't better than me, and if you plan on crushing my writing 'cause I don't bow down and kiss your fucking feet, then you can shove all of it."

I turned to leave and didn't even notice he'd gotten up out of his seat. When I turned around, just about to blow my final gasket, he took my face gently in his hands and said, "Yes."

I couldn't for the life of me understand what he was saying yes to.

"Yes, what?"

He smiled, the crooked way people do when they're being a little ornery. "You asked me if I'm interested in you for more than just the books you write, and the answer is yes. It might be stupid, could be inappropriate, but the answer is still yes."

I stared at him for a long moment and, still on an adrenaline high, reached up and pulled him down to me, crushing my mouth into his. He returned my kiss with equal passion, the two of us tangled into each other, when Irene cleared her throat.

I pulled back so fast and so far that I bumped into the wall of books that stood next to the doorway.

Irene was obviously trying not to smile, and she kept her head bowed. When I looked at Liam, his face was glowing red, but his eyes were on me like an animal about to attack its prey.

I pulled in a breath as Irene said, "Your lunch appointment is here," and darted out the door.

"Fuck." I said in a whisper, afraid the person he was meeting next would hear me. I was just about to leave when an older woman walked into the room. She was tall and thin, the perfect mix of New York sophistication. Her hair was coiffed beautifully and the aroma that came in with her was intense and expensive.

She looked over at Liam, then at me, and cocked her eyebrow in the same way Liam usually did.

Fuck, it's his mother. Of course, it's his mother.

"Well, Mr. Rickard," I quickly recovered. "I think that pretty much covers my questions."

Even saying that made me blush, and when the woman noticed she laughed out loud. I had visions of Christine Baranski on *The Good Fight* right before she filleted someone.

"I'll leave you to your next appointment," I said, ready to run like a scared child from the room.

"Oh, no you're not," she said, stopping me dead in my tracks. "I see I've come at an inopportune time, which, of course, is a mother's greatest achievement. Mister..."

She waited for me to give her my name.

"Devereaux," I said, ready to wilt and die.

Her eyes grew big and she looked over at her son, who was clearly equally mortified. Which, truthfully, gave me more satisfaction than it should have.

"You are Mr. Bobby Devereaux, star writer of our latest books?" she asked. "That's lovely," she purred and looked back at Liam. "I'm sure your father will be very pleased. Mr. Devereaux, it would be a huge honor if you'd join us for lunch. Wouldn't it, darling?"

I thought about it for a minute, then just for the perverse enjoyment of watching Liam squirm, I said, "I *am* a bit hungry."

When Liam looked at me, I could tell he was ready to strangle both of us. His mother laughed again.

I looked down at what I was wearing and sighed.

"I'm afraid I'm not really dressed for going out, though. I was trying on these clothes when I..." I hadn't thought that through. I'd stormed over here ready to give Liam a piece of my mind, not to go to lunch at a fancy restaurant.

The woman's smile continued to glow. She was enjoying this as much as I was. "Well, where we are going, designer tees and jeans are perfect as long as you remove those tags, of course."

I blushed and walked past her, asking Irene for scissors.

She pulled a pair out of her desk, snipped the offending tags off, and tossed them. Then she whispered to me, "I haven't seen that man off his game this much since I met him. Keep it up, it's good for him."

I chuckled. "I think I've just met my match with this one, though. Oh, what's her name?" I whispered.

"I'm Tiffany Rickard," Liam's mother said. "No need for Mrs. or anything like that. Just Tiffany will do."

I blushed at getting caught asking the question and reached over to take the woman's hand in my own.

"It is a genuine pleasure Mrs....I mean, Tiffany."

She smiled and I knew now where Liam's crooked and mischievous smile came from. I felt like prey caught between a lion and an eagle as both Tiffany and her son looked at me. I liked it when she made her son squirm, but I wasn't a big fan when that was turned on me.

Tiffany led us to the garage elevator, and when the doors opened, a limo was waiting for us. The driver opened the door and Tiffany slipped in first. I looked at Liam, who was staring at me with the same intensity as before. To avoid having to examine my reaction to that, I slipped into the car next to his mom.

"It's my understanding that you live on a farm in Iowa," she said.

I smiled, wondering what it must be like for a New York elite to see her son flirting with a low-life farmer.

"Yes, we have over ten thousand hogs working at the moment." I saw her blanch a bit and thought, *score one for me.*

She recovered quickly enough and asked, "So, what do you do on the farm?"

I laughed. "It's my brother's farm now. When I help out, I'm free labor."

"How often do you offer such generous help?" she asked.

"Whenever I'm home," I replied honestly. "It's better than using a gym and I get free food in the form of my mom's cooking when I'm done."

She smiled and I could tell we were on a topic that she felt much more comfortable with as she asked me questions about my mom and the rest of my family.

By the time we got to the restaurant, I felt like I'd just completed an interrogation with the Inquisition and lived to tell about it.

The limo pulled up in front of Times Square's *Hunt and Fish Club* and I sighed with relief. I'd been here before with Randy. It was business casual, not too snooty. The food was good, too.

We were seated right away, which didn't surprise me. The *A-listers*, as I called the NYC elite, tended to have their favorite restaurants well-trained.

Luckily, after we were seated, the conversation drifted away from me and onto Liam. Mostly it was typical mom stuff. *Are you eating right? When was the last time you took some time for yourself?*

It was heartening to see that the inquisition I'd just received was this woman's natural way and didn't have anything to do with me personally.

Once we'd discussed my being a farmer, I'd expected the cold shoulder. I'd experienced it enough hanging with Randy. It hadn't really bothered me, though. Still, the fact that she hadn't given me the cold shoulder did give her some diplomacy credits in my mind.

Occasionally, Tiffany would steer the conversation back to me. At one point, she made some comment about the tuna being a travesty. "I just wish they'd leave that off the menu."

I couldn't resist. "Why do you feel that way?" I asked, expecting it to be something about not being pure enough or some bourgeoisie crap.

She looked at me seriously and said, "We are overfishing our oceans. The tuna is a predator fish essential for the equilibrium of the ocean habitat. It's as destructive to kill tuna as it is to kill sharks."

I was shocked. In all my time among Randy's associates and friends, not a single one of them had acted like they gave a damn about the environment.

I leaned in closer. "I can't agree more. It drives me insane how no one seems to care or notice."

Seeing as we'd found our common ground, I asked her what she thought of the polar ice caps melting, and Liam rolled his eyes. The remainder of the time, we talked about climate change and the impact it was having on the environment.

She and I were having such a good time talking that we chatted for another hour after Liam took a cab back to the office.

"I like you, Tiffany," I finally said after we left the restaurant and were sitting at a cute little bistro not far from the hotel.

She smiled. "I like you, too. But clearly not nearly as much as my son does."

I blushed. "I don't know about that. He and I have a sort of love-hate thing going on."

"Oh, those are the best ones," she said with a wicked smile.

I just shook my head. "Anyway, I'm only here for the Comic-Con debut of the next book. Then I'm back to the farm."

"I heard all about that farm," she said, and when I raised my eyebrows, she laughed out loud. "My perfectly put-together son in a pile of poo. I've laughed about that for months. It's good for him to get his hands dirty. I tried when he was young, but there just wasn't much opportunity for that in New York. He wasn't really into horseback riding and his father wouldn't let me loan him out to pick up trash in Central Park..."

I looked at her funny. "You'll have to forgive me, but I've been around New York's elite for a while, and you are definitely not fitting the profile."

"I didn't grow up in New York. I grew up on a vineyard in the South of France."

I was shocked. "Where's the accent?"

"Well disguised," she moaned. "I learned when I married my husband that anything that made you different was considered a character flaw. Even a French accent could make me stand out and possibly give the petty people we had to schmooze for the business ammunition to hurt my husband's career. Of course, that was then. Things are different now. The in-crowd doesn't have as much control as they did when I moved here."

"Still, a vineyard in southern France is a far cry from a hog farm in Iowa. I was a pariah when I was here before. Hell, I'm still surprised my boyfriend at the time would let me out of the house."

She nodded. "Well, he isn't known for his discretion," she said.

When I looked shocked at her statement, she shrugged and said, "You think someone like you would escape the attention of the busybodies around here? When you dumped him and then hit it big, you were the talk of the town. Randy is an ass. It's amazing he gets invited to any events."

"I figured he'd tell everyone the lies that caused us to break up."

"Oh, he did," she said, winking at me. "But the guy that you messaged on Facebook—the one you told to let Randy know you were leaving—he's the son of the second-richest man in New York. Total brat, but he loves to gossip, so he filled everyone in on what you'd said. That's how we all knew Randy was full of it."

I sighed. "I still have no idea why that arrogant bag of wind told him all those lies anyway. Randy begged me to stay...no, never mind." I put my hands up to stop myself. "I haven't thought of that guy in a long time. Let's just say I'm happy to be away from him."

She smiled and the mischievous glint slipped into her eyes again as she took another sip of her coffee.

"Would you like to screw with him a little?" she asked.

"Not really. I want to forget he exists."

"Ah, you're no fun," she pouted. "Just when I thought I had a co-conspirator I could be naughty with."

"Okay, because naughty sounds fun, I'm open. What's your idea?"

She smiled. "I'm throwing a Save the Ocean gala this Saturday night. He's coming." Mirth twinkled in her eyes. "If you were on the arm of a very handsome, eligible bachelor—whom I know he has the hots for— say, like my very handsome son, Liam, for example, it would eat him alive."

I shook my head. "No. I don't have anything formal to wear and I've spent all the money I'm willing to spend on ridiculously expensive clothes. Besides, I don't want to use Liam to get back at my ex. That seems wrong."

"You look like you're my husband's size, you can wear something of his. He'll never know. He's as vain as Liam and has more Armani than the Armanis themselves. You can go as my guest if you don't want to pull Liam into this. It would still tick him off, just you being there."

"Oh, Tiffany, I swore I'd never go to another one of those horrible things. No offense."

She sighed. "None taken and I understand. I wouldn't go myself if I wasn't hosting the damned thing."

Just then her French accent slipped into the conversation and I smiled. I'd managed to fluff out the real person after all.

"Were you just inviting me as a distraction?" I asked.

She nodded. "I'll admit watching Randy's face would almost make it worth dealing with that crowd."

"Okay, I'll come," I said on the spur of the moment. "But I'm not wearing your husband's suit. I have a friend who is my size, and he has all that fancy stuff. I'll go raid his closet."

She clapped her hands and then scooted over to side hug me.

"But you owe me, seriously. I'm going to collect one day too!"

She crossed her heart and said, "Ask, and I will do my best to pay you back."

Tiffany dropped me off at the hotel. When I got to my room, I checked my phone, which I'd left plugged into the wall. Coverage at home wasn't consistent, so I'd got over the need to have my phone on me twenty-four-seven.

No surprise, I had several texts from Liam.

I texted him back.

Sorry, your mom just dropped me off. She's so cool. What happened to you?

He sent me back an angry face emoji, which made me laugh.

Can you join me for dinner? He asked.

Maybe. Better yet, let's meet somewhere to talk. I still have questions. The kiss and your mom sort of messed up that conversation.

He wrote back saying he'd meet me in the hotel bar after six. I hadn't thought of that, but it was a good idea. The bar had been mostly empty since I'd arrived, the music wasn't too loud, and the atmosphere was laid-back.

Perfect. Six in the bar.

I had a few hours before I was scheduled to meet him, so I plopped back onto the bed. My mind, as it was accustomed to doing, began animating the scenes from my day.

I'd really liked Tiffany. She was like a superhero in that she had a persona that in no way represented the awesome woman underneath.

Her stance on climate change and the environment gave me the idea for a character who worked in politics as a well-known philanthropist and all-round ass-kicking woman, all the while secretly protecting the world against evil as a superhero.

It took me a moment to figure out how to represent climate change in a way that would interest readers. Suddenly, I had an epiphany and sat up.

I grabbed my computer and began describing a new monster, which morphed into various human-created catastrophes at will. Just like Godzilla representing the horrors of nuclear war, this monster represented the horrors of sewage and plastics in the oceans, overfishing, and global warming.

Our heroine was the only one that could stand up to it. But of course, she couldn't succeed by herself. That's why she had to play the role of politician and influencer. Her job as a superhero was to protect the city when the monster came in the form of a hurricane or other natural disaster.

I was buried in thought when my phone pinged. I was about to ignore it, but thought, *no, it could be Mom or Dad.*

Dad had been feeling off lately and I didn't want to not be available if they needed me.

I looked at the phone and saw it was from Liam. Shit, it was six-fifteen.

Sorry, Liam, I got caught up writing. I'll be right down.

I rushed out of the room, thanking the Universe I hadn't changed out of my clothes from earlier.

When I got to the bar, I saw Liam sitting with his back against the far wall. I rushed over and quickly kissed his lips before scooting up next to him. I hadn't even noticed I'd pushed a social boundary. I was still stuck in the world of the novel I'd started.

I began telling him how his mom had inspired me and about the creature I created to represent all things evil that humans had thrust upon the world. He just stared at me as I went on and on.

Finally, a server came over for our drink orders, and when I looked at Liam it hit me that I just let the cat out of the bag. I'd basically given away everything I'd meant to keep to myself until I knew if the new book was going to be accepted or not.

I sighed. "Just a ginger ale for me."

Liam looked at me inquisitively and told the server, "I'll have a gin and tonic."

I looked down and said, "I didn't mean to tell you I was writing again. Can you pretend like I didn't get caught up in the heat of the moment?"

When I looked up at him, he was smiling.

"I knew you couldn't resist," he said and leaned over to plant a delicious, sweet-but-possessive kiss on me.

"So, here's the deal. I've made no promises. If this new book flops—and it could, 'cause it isn't anything like the other—I won't be pursuing another book. Your mom just inspired me today, that's all. She's so perfectly coiffed and aristocratic. Then, just when you think you have her figured out, poof! She's the massive environmentalist holding a gala to save the ocean. Which really is to save the ocean, not just to impress her stupid, stuck-up friends. I haven't told anyone I'm thinking about writing more, not even Doug, so on this you're gonna have to be boyfriend Liam, not CEO Liam. Got it?"

"I want more than a kiss before I commit to being your boyfriend, Bobby."

I blushed. "I didn't mean..."

He blocked me with a kiss before pulling back. "I know what you meant."

I sighed deeply and pushed back in my seat. "Maybe I do need a drink, although I'd prefer to avoid it and just go back upstairs and write."

"Why don't you hold off? Have a drink and talk with me. You'll be back in bumfuck Iowa—and I don't mean that the good way—next week and can huddle up in that nightmare house of yours and write to your heart's content. But for now, I'd like to spend time with you."

I pouted. "My house isn't a nightmare. You saw it just after I bought it. I hadn't had time to do many renovations. It's actually really cute now, and it has heat!"

He smiled at me and took my hand, kissing it. "I'm sure it's adorable, pig shit and all."

I pulled my hand back. "You're being offensive."

"Well, a little. But it's not like you didn't have it coming, tossing me in a pile of pig shit after making me sleep in an icebox on a mattress they used during the Middle Ages to torture people."

"Hey, if I remember right, you arrived unannounced and decided to stay even though I hadn't invited you. All I had was that mattress, and I was sleeping in the icebox too, blockhead. Besides, I didn't push you into that poo. You fell, and I wrote you what could end up being a multi-million-dollar novel as an apology, so we're even."

He laughed out loud. "You are so different from anyone I've ever known. I swear that should turn me off but clearly, I'm a glutton for punishment. Bobby, I can't seem to get enough of you."

I paused a moment, gathering my thoughts. "It seemed like you've been avoiding me like the plague." I said thinking of the première and his less than attentive reaction to seeing me."

"No, I've avoided Iowa like the plague. You were just unfortunately located there."

"Okay, truce on the Iowa stuff. It's a great state and I love it. You didn't get to see the best of it. The hog farm is difficult to get used to even if you grew up on it, so don't be blaming Iowa for Devereaux Farms."

"Noted. Maybe I'll give you a chance to show me the good stuff, especially if you have a new book in the works."

"Nah," I said. "CEO Liam can't know anything about the book. You gotta keep him in the dark."

He laughed. "I've never been good at compartmentalizing."

"Well, high time you learned," I said, not giving an inch. "Besides, if you can learn not to put pressure on me, I'll fill you in on some of my ideas. But only as someone I'm slightly interested in dating."

"Slightly?"

"Slightly, but if you can be a friend too, that could increase the interest substantially."

He put his arm around me. "I'd like the friendship, too," he said.

I smiled and snuggled into his side.

I'm not sure what it was about this man. Maybe his big frame, maybe his handsome features, or the fact I seemed to keep him totally off-balance. But I wanted to keep touching him all the time. I wasn't overly affectionate. In fact, even when I got serious with someone, Randy, for example, I tended to be more standoffish than touchy-feely. Randy had even mentioned it a few times, and I'd just said it was because I was from Iowa. Truth was, I hadn't really wanted to snuggle with Randy.

I didn't seem to be able to stop around Liam, though. Be it wanting to have my arm in his as we walked down the sidewalks or having my hand on his as he drove down the road, I just seemed to feel right when I was touching him.

Of course, this all made me think about how pleasurable making love with him would be.

"So, what was it you wanted to talk to me about?" he asked.

"Well, that's a CEO conversation. You mind putting friend Liam to the side for a moment?"

"I don't want to, but if it helps to get this out of the way."

"It does."

"Okay. CEO Liam at your service."

"So, Doug said something that got me to thinking. You have a lot of power over me since you're the CEO of my publishing company."

He nodded.

"I know we're skirting some legal shit, so I won't ask you to incriminate yourself or make promises or anything like that, but if you and I try this and it doesn't work out, can you tell me with confidence you won't use that against me? Or, more importantly, against my work?"

He leaned back, studied his nails. I could tell he was thinking through the legal stuff. "Well, yes and no. If we date and it falls apart, I'm still going to be CEO. I won't promise I can compartmentalize my feelings for someone from my professional career, be those good or bad. What I can and will do, though, if we decide we're gonna try to date, is set out a few parameters. Kind of like a prenuptial agreement, but a predating agreement. If we split up and you keep writing, I can hand your stuff to someone else to handle. Besides, it isn't like others don't handle most of it anyway."

I leaned back and thought about that for a moment. "Better deal. Let someone else handle everything anyway. You've moved Roy up fast enough, why not give him my account? I like him, he likes me. He is a fucking drill sergeant about my edits, which is what I need. And you won't have to be involved, at least not directly."

He looked at me for a long moment, then said, "I like being involved."

"Well, silly, if we're dating, you will be involved but not in my livelihood. This way, if I fuck up professionally, Roy can dump me without it impacting our relationship. And if you and I split up, and my sales are still doing well, then I don't have to worry about you sabotaging my career."

"How do you know you can trust me?" he asked.

"Because you may be a monster to work for, but everyone has always said you are fair and honest. I trust you 'cause other people have vouched for you."

He shook his head. "You're asking a lot. You are the only client I keep tabs on. I consider you my pet project. You may not know this, but I really went out on a limb with your book. We weren't a graphic novel publisher, and we normally focus more on romance than fantasy. It worked out and helped pull my first year as CEO out of the toilet, so I have a vested interest in you professionally."

I shrugged. "I'm afraid you need to decide. I need to feel at least that I've got some protection here if we move forward with whatever this is."

After another moment of thought, he reached his hand over for a shake.

"Deal," he said when I took it. "I'll have Roy take your account over starting next week, after Comic-Con."

"Do I still get to go to Tokyo?" I asked, and he laughed.

"Everything we've decided up to this point will stay the same."

"Okay," I said and reached over to kiss him on the mouth. "Now, back to the good stuff."

Liam Rickard

The man truly overwhelmed me. When he showed up in my office, angry and almost literally puffing smoke out of his ears, I didn't expect to end up passionately kissing him. And that was before my mom walked in.

Then when he didn't show up at the bar right at six, I felt myself becoming angrier and angrier, thinking he was playing with me. He didn't seem like a player or a manipulator, but the hog shit incident kept looping around in my brain, at least until I shut it off and texted him.

He showed up within moments. Then he kissed me like we were a couple, which made all the mad completely deflate. He began going on and on about his new character and how my mom had inspired him, and a little part of the steel cage I'd built around my heart fell away. He liked my mom. Nobody I dated liked my mom. They liked my dad, who was a hard-ass with great advice about how to invest your money, but Mom was intense, rarely opening up to anyone about the things she loved. When she did, it was usually in a way that left the person she was talking to feeling judged.

Mom was passionate, full of life, and she loved me with her entire being. Because of her, I had no doubt my father had learned to be an okay dad. Through her, he and I learned to tolerate each other.

To have someone who liked her, not because of me or because of something she could do for them well, that warmed my heart to its core.

The fact Bobby had been inspired by her was maybe more than my little heart could even consider for the moment.

The friendship thing also struck a chord with me. I'd always known that what made my parents' relationship work was the fact that the two of them were friends first and lovers, spouses, and parents next. I'd said since I was a teenager that I would have to be friends with the man I married, or I'd never get married.

All was good until he told me he wanted me to hand the account over to Roy. I'd held onto this account since the first story had landed on my desk. It saved me as CEO and frankly, it had saved the company as well, giving us a new direction that had brought us real success.

He was right and I knew it. However, it was tough to let this one go. Then I thought of how wonderful he felt up against me and how it would feel to have him under me, and I relented. I appreciated his faith in me, but I wasn't at all sure I had that kind of self-control. Time would tell.

We walked around New York that night. Bobby wrapped up against me like he had been the day before when we'd walked around Little Italy and Chinatown. We wandered through Times Square, up to the Broadway theaters and then back to the hotel, genuinely enjoying each other's company.

"I'm not sure I've ever enjoyed just being around someone as much as I enjoy being around you," I said.

He smiled up at me. "Me too, but I bet it's gonna be better, in that way."

I almost lost my breath. I had to force myself not to pull him into a dark alley and fuck him. The way he kept touching me set off sexual sparks inside my body.

When we finally walked back into his hotel, I literally pulled him to the elevator and hit the button fifteen times, trying to get it to speed up. Once the door closed, I pulled him into a kiss, deep and passionate. Who gave a fuck if security was watching?

He managed to get his key out and both of us through the door before I began stripping him.

I began sucking on his silky skin as I exposed each inch.

"I can't remember wanting anyone this much," I whispered.

Bobby moaned deliciously as I explored his neck with my tongue.

"I want you too, Liam." When I bit down on his pulse point, he sucked in a breath and rasped, "I want you so fucking much."

I immediately pushed him down on the bed, surprising myself at how aggressive I was being. Usually, my sexual experiences had been detached and controlled, never heated like this. And I had never pushed anyone onto a bed before. But Bobby always seemed to put me off my game and evidently, sex wasn't going to be any different.

I knelt over his trembling body and licked between his pecs up to his Adam's apple.

"You taste good," I moaned and went back down to take his nipple in my mouth before he could respond.

"Fuck!" he growled, writhing under me and causing the lust inside me to become even stronger.

I quickly undid his belt while I continued sucking his nipple. When I slipped my hand into his jeans, grabbing his cock, I bit down on his nipple until I drew a strangled cry from him.

I knew I was pushing him, but I desperately wanted him to be as out of control as I was.

I moved down to his abs, enjoying how they contracted when my tongue brushed over them. I finished undoing his pants, pulling them off. Taking his cock into my mouth through his underwear I felt perverse joy shoot through me as Bobby all but yelled my name before falling back onto the bed.

I looked up at him. A strange control took over me on the outside while I quivered on the inside.

"You like that?" I whispered.

Bobby's eyes were clouded with lust as he nodded in response to my question.

I rubbed my hand over his crotch as I waited for his answer, knowing I was undoing the man with my touch and perversely enjoying it more than I probably should.

"Good," I said, pulling his cock out of his underwear and licking the precum that was leaking from the tip.

"Fuck, that's so...that's so..." he started to say as I took the head of his cock into my mouth.

I looked up at him, making eye contact as I sucked hard. I popped the head out of my mouth and let it fall back onto his abdomen.

"You have a delicious cock," I said.

Before he could respond, I sucked him back into my mouth and deep into my throat before swallowing.

He moaned loudly, which just prompted me to suck him more, suck him harder.

When he began to buck into my mouth, I knew I had him where I wanted him.

Bobby Devereaux

Liam's sexual aggression was just what I needed. I let him take complete control and fuck, if that wasn't making me a puddle of raw need.

When he took my cock in his mouth, watching me all the while, I thought I might scream.

He sucked me until I was fucking his mouth, and that's when I was done letting him run the show.

I moved under him, pushing him onto his back and straddling his face. He eagerly took me back into his mouth as I leaned over, taking his cock into my mouth. Driven by the vibration of his moans, I fucked him as I sucked him deep into my throat.

When his moans increased, I fucked his mouth harder. He'd already shown he could take a cock deep when he'd taken me into his mouth and swallowed, so I knew he could handle my girth.

His cock was long and thick, and it was the perfect size to suck. Liam squirmed under me, freeing his hands, which he then used to jack me off when he took a breath. His fingers, wet with saliva, moved up until they reached my hole and he began teasing the puckered skin. The sensation sent electric pulses through my body and I sat up and cried out his name.

I wasn't one to go for anal sex the first time I hooked up with someone, but when he began to play with my hole, I thought I might lose all control. No doubt, Liam would be able to pry anything he wanted out of me at this point.

"Oh, fuck!" I whimpered as his finger breached my hole for the first time. "Fuck, Liam, that feels so fucking good."

I sat up, pulling my cock from his mouth, and settled my ass over his face instead. Liam immediately got the message, his tongue swiping across my pucker before pushing inside. I couldn't help but thrust against the intrusion, riding his tongue with abandon.

I was moaning like a crazy person and he attacked me as if he was starving.

He pulled back just enough to say, "Bobby, you taste so good. I want to fuck you, though. Can I fuck you?"

The answer in any other situation would be *hell no*. I don't fuck anyone on the first date. But he slid his tongue inside my loosening hole, demonstrating with that talented appendage what he proposed doing with his cock. I couldn't resist.

"Please, please..."

Liam took control again, pushing me off him and reaching into his pants which were down around his knees. He pulled out a condom and a small packet of lube.

I took them from him and sucked his cock again as I took the condom out of its wrapping. Liam fucked my mouth until I pulled off him and rolled the condom onto his throbbing cock.

He laughed mischievously. "Lay on your back. I want to watch your face while we do this."

I did as I was instructed. After removing his pants, Liam moved between my legs, opened the lube, and began slipping a finger inside me, using it to prep me and loosen me more. I writhed under his touch, enjoying the sensation. When he slipped the second finger in, I sucked in a breath, enjoying the sensation of pain and pleasure so completely tied together.

"You're so tight, you sure you want to do this?" he asked.

"Fuck yeah, I really wanna do this. Goddamn, Liam, I need this. I need you in me."

Laughing again, softly this time, he smeared his cock with lube and pressed it against my opening, the broad head stretching that ring of muscle, breaching me. Pain warred with pleasure and I moaned. "Slow...go slow." My voice quivered, breathless as the sting pulsed through me. "It's been a while."

He left his cockhead inside me and leaned over for a kiss. The tenderness after his aggression almost undid me.

I began to push back against him and Liam shuddered. I could tell he was having a hard time not just taking me all at once.

I wrapped my legs around him and pulled myself further and further onto his cock, which was bigger than I was used to. When he was all the way in, I held him with one hand until the burn subsided and was quickly replaced by pleasure. He leaned over and kissed me again, this time lingering, biting my lower lip before he moved slightly, his movements now teasing me with the promise of pleasure.

"Fuck," I yelled. "You gotta fuck me! Fuck me now, Liam!"

I could feel his smile against my mouth, the heat from it searing my lips.

He thrust into me, his cock swelling as he watched my face while he took me. I bucked with the pleasure of finally having him inside me after wanting it so desperately.

"Goddamn, you feel so good," he growled.

"All...please!" I begged, unable to get out a complete sentence but knowing he understood because he immediately plunged his cock fully into me. My back bowed at the intense pleasure.

He fucked me harder and harder, watching me. His heated stare consumed me, owned me.

"Fuck, oh fuck! That feels good! I want you in me! Fuck me harder, Liam!"

He complied. His skin slapping against mine.

Liam shifted then and hit my prostate. I moaned with the intensity of the sensation.

"Fuck! I'm gonna come!"

"Yeah, come for me, baby!" Liam cried as he continued ramming my prostate.

My orgasm crashed over me and I exploded, coating my abdomen and chest, even hitting the headboard behind us. I was about to laugh at that when Liam leaned over and crushed my mouth with his. He came that way, moaning his ecstasy into my mouth as the warm ribbons of his release spilled inside the condom.

He pulled back, his body jerking, and fell next to me.

We laid together in the afterglow, both of us still breathing heavily.

"God, I needed that," I said, and Liam laughed beside me.

"Yeah, me too."

I curled against his side and snuggled into him. He took the condom off while I enjoyed the sensation of him pressed against me. He rolled back over and wrapped his arms around me.

"I'm not sure I've ever been fucked that good...well, not in a long time," I said.

Liam chuckled, and I felt the vibration through my body as he held me. "We can do it again. I'm sure it'll get even better with some practice."

I leaned up and smiled. "We get to do it again?"

"I fucking hope so!" he exclaimed, making me laugh.

We continued to lay like that, both of us falling asleep as the afterglow embraced us.

Finally, Liam shifted and went to the en suite. He came back with a warm, wet towel and began cleaning me up.

The gentleness he used now was such a contrast to the aggressive way he'd taken me. It was overwhelmingly sweet.

When he finished and tossed the towel into the en suite, he lay back down next to me.

I leaned up on my elbow, tracing my finger along his beautifully sculpted face.

"So, you're French, huh?" I asked.

He laughed. "No, my mom is French. I'm a New Yorker."

I lay back down and stared up at the ceiling. "You know this is a royally bad idea, right?"

He shook his head. "You suck at pillow talk." Then he ribbed me a little, causing me to squirm.

"No, I don't think it is. I think dancing around each other like we have for the past few months has been a bad idea. This feels like..." He hesitated, choosing his words. "Like the most right thing we've done."

He got up and headed toward the shower. "Well, besides your writing and me publishing your bestselling kick-ass novel from heaven."

I didn't immediately follow him into the shower. I lay where I was, thinking about what he'd just said. Was he doing all this just so I'd keep writing? He'd convinced me...no, I'd convinced myself to write the second novel because I'd screwed up. Apparently, I was going to write this next book because I wanted to. But I had to wonder if him hooking up with me had more to do with getting another book out of me than him liking me. That would be a New York Executive CEO thing to do.

I shook the thought out of my head.

Even if he was being manipulative, you like him, I told myself.

Hell, I could barely keep my hands off him. That tall bronze body, more legs than torso, beautifully sculpted back. Just thinking about him made my cock begin to fill again.

"Fuck it," I said and went to join him in the shower. I'd rather enjoy the show than lose the chance.

When I slipped in behind him, Liam purred at my touch. He turned around and began soaping me up, rubbing all the parts we'd just used, causing my cock to harden even more. He washed my ass, letting his finger rub my hole and slip in just enough to send me into ecstasy again.

I was throbbing by the time he began to rinse us both off. He hung the showerhead back up and, positioning me so the water hit my back and shielded him, he knelt and took my cock back into his mouth.

This time, instead of taking me with intensity, he moved slowly, savoring the moment. I moaned as he continued to fuck his mouth with my cock. I wanted him inside me, but knowing I was nowhere near ready to be fucked again, I pulled him up and switched places with him, taking his cock into my mouth while stroking my own.

When I sucked him back into my throat and swallowed like he'd done with me earlier, he immediately began to thrust into my mouth.

"I'm going to come," he said, and I began to suck him harder, suddenly delirious at the thought of him exploding in my mouth.

His release hit the back of my throat, causing me to gag. How could he come that much so soon after coming in my ass?

My body was on fire. Knowing I'd created so much pleasure in him that he came twice, each time with such intensity. I came again, shooting cum across the shower floor, although not nearly as much as he had.

Liam pulled me up and crushed his mouth to mine. The fact that I knew he tasted himself on me almost made me hard again. I had a distinct cum kink, and it appeared he did too.

We washed up again and dried off before crashing into the big hotel bed. I'm not ashamed to say two incredible bouts of sex put me right to sleep. The fact that Liam spooned me as I dozed off was just an incredible addition to an already amazing night.

***

Eddie, my frenemy, met me at his door. He looked me up and down and apparently approved of my new designer apparel.

"You've turned over a new leaf," he said with a sneer.

"No, not really. I just had to have something for all these Comic-Cons I'm doing."

"Well, come on in," he sighed. As I walked in, he said, under his breath, but loud enough that I could hear, "You can take the man out of Iowa..."

"Well, glad to see you're still a bitch." I replied, getting a glare from him.

Eddie had been the first person I'd met when I came to New York— Grindr date gone terribly wrong. He'd walked in swishing his body with as much drama as he could, looked me up and down, and said, "I'd rather fuck the dog."

He'd been about to leave when I'd said, "More like pig farmer."

I have no idea why I didn't just let his diva ass walk out. Maybe because I was scared and lonely being in a new place.

He'd turned around and said, "Well, that explains all this," as he waved his hand up and down my body. "Walmart special isn't gonna cut it here, baby, but never mind. I can help you."

That's when he dragged me across the city to his apartment in Battery Park. The moment we stepped off the subway, he began telling me about all the famous people who lived in the area.

"Tyra Banks just sold her apartment there." He pointed toward a building to our right. "For seventeen mil."

This went on until I was nauseated with the name-dropping.

"Do you always do that?" I asked when we were headed upstairs to his apartment.

"Do what, darling?" he asked.

"Name-drop, like all these famous people are somehow boosting your social standing?"

"Of course, darling. I pay out the nose for this place. They are boosting my social standing."

When we got to his apartment—which was actually a bit smaller than mine, but in a much more desirable part of town—we walked into, well, it was a closet in many ways. Small and full of clothing.

"Fuck," I said as I looked around, and of course, he took that as a compliment, whether it was meant to be or not.

"Yes!" he said and literally twirled around the room like some ten-year-old ballerina. "My creation!"

I was speechless. Eddie walked past the clothes, and as he did, his hand rubbed across them, like he was petting a beloved animal.

"I was almost on America's Next Top Model," he said. "I was almost there and got pneumonia chasing some stupid man who'd dumped me for a younger...well, model."

I looked at him like he was insane.

"Was the other man a child?" I asked. The man didn't look a day over nineteen himself.

Eddie threw back his head and laughed. "That earns you points, darling, major points."

He pulled me to the back of his clothes closet apartment, pushed a few racks out of the way, and found a box he'd thrown a bunch of stuff into.

"There, that's your box. And my contribution to society."

I should've been offended. Clearly, he was offering me his castoffs like he was donating to the Salvation Army. I wasn't going to say anything because I loved thrift stores. Being an avowed environmentalist, I was completely dedicated to using stuff people had discarded and saving some poor ten-year-old in a developing nation from having to make any clothes for me. But the more I thought about it, the more I thought I'm not a fucking charity case.

"Dude, I don't need your castoffs," I said and turned to leave.

"Bullshit," he said. He pulled me over toward the box and began stripping me.

"What the hell?" I asked, fighting to keep my shirt on.

He looked at me oddly. "We were about to hook up, now you're gonna be shy?" he asked.

"Well, yeah, especially after you rejected me," I replied, holding my shirt down.

He laughed. "Okay, suit yourself. I'll leave you to it. But put on something from that box and come find me. I'll be in the kitchen."

He left with a swish, and I shrugged. I'd followed the clearly insane man all the way here. What could it hurt to placate him? Besides, I was a little curious.

The box was full of beautiful clothes. I recognized the names and sneered at the labels. Several of the brands were made in parts of the world that were known for using child labor. I avoided those, found a shirt and a pair of pants that were known for being ethically made. Eddie and I were apparently the exact same size. How was that even possible?

I went to find him.

When I walked out, he exclaimed, "Perfect." He spun me around and looked at me. "I should've known you'd pick out the Massimo Dutti pants. They were the cheapest thing in there."

He shook his head and headed off to find me a pair of shoes. Again, I was surprised to find they fit so well.

"Next thing is the hair."

I had to rush back to grab my keys and wallet from my pants as he dragged me out the door. Before I knew it, I was sitting in a chair at a swanky salon, getting my hair done. I knew I needed a haircut. After leaving the university two months earlier, I'd spent some time running around with friends, and we hadn't done much other than going swimming or drinking at a local bar.

When I got the job offer from the paper, I came straight out without doing much other than packing. When the stylist was done, I looked ridiculous. My hair was standing straight up and had been tapered on the sides and back. I might look like I'd just walked off the runway, but the style didn't match my personality at all. When I said as much, both the stylist, Sabastian, and Eddie laughed and said that was exactly what they were going for.

I don't think I'd have stuck with it, except every head turned as we walked down Pearl Street. Eddie smiled as I tugged at my clothes uncomfortably.

"If you wanted, I could probably introduce you to a few modeling agents. You seem to have an eye-catching look...when you toss off the ugly."

"No thank you," I said, ignoring the looks as we walked back toward Eddie's place so I could collect my stuff.

When I was dressed to his standards, he and I enjoyed hanging out. Nothing sexual ever happened between us, but he was my go-to person when I needed help dressing for some big meeting or social event. When I was shacked up with Randy, Eddie had kept me above the social fray. As a result, despite his prickly personality, I found a special place in my heart for him. Still, we'd both tell you the friendship was tenuous at best.

Eddie was quick to pull out a Saint Laurent tux and matching Christian Louboutin shoes pulling me back into the present.

"What did this cost?" I asked him as he was helping me with the shoes.

"There are two things you aren't supposed to ask me, Devereaux, my age and what I spend on clothing. All you need to know is if you scuff those shoes, I'm going to reconsider our platonic relationship and take it out of your ass."

I laughed. "You're such an ass, Eddie. Why are you dressing me up so much today? You usually take me to the back and make me pick out stuff from your castaway box."

He sighed. "I don't like how that douchebag treated you. You may be a hick, but you have a good character. I heard some of the shit he said about you and, well, if I hadn't been afraid I'd ruin my manicure, I'd have busted his fucking nose."

I wanted to ask for details but decided it was best that I didn't know. Randy and Eddie had known each other through various gay parties and uppity events that made my stomach hurt when I thought about them. I really did hate those parties.

So, to change the subject, I asked, "How did you know I was going to see him?"

Eddie, in a way that was always endearing, leaned back and laughed out loud.

"Baby, I know everything about everything in this city."

"Whatever," I said, but secretly I was always impressed at how Eddie did seem to have his finger on the pulse of this vast town.

"I know you hate this kind of shit. If you weren't going to be able to throw your success in his face, I know for a fact you wouldn't be going."

"Touché," I replied. "It sucks that you know me so well."

"You aren't very mysterious, baby," Eddie said as he pushed me back and looked me over.

"Let's go see Sabastian and get that mop styled. Randy won't know what hit him."

Sabastian became the only stylist I ever saw in New York. He was on the other side of the city from me and cost way more than I could afford, but I figured when in Rome...

Unlike Eddie, who was a snob, Sabastian was much more down-to-earth. He'd grown up in rural Georgia and moved to New York after he graduated from beauty school. He was an artist with hair and as a result, he'd quickly risen in the world of modeling. His more country roots, however, allowed us to become good friends. So I'd already intended to go see him anyway while I was in the city.

He took one look at the tux and whistled.

"Oh my, I never thought of you as someone I'd fuck," he said with a wink. "But I might have to reconsider."

"Oh great, now both you and Eddie are reconsidering a fuck with me after all this time. Maybe we should just have a *ménage à trois* right here on the floor," I said with as much sarcasm as I could muster.

"You'd be so lucky," Sabastian said as he shoved me into the chair and tore into my hair. "Give your jacket to Eddie. I don't want to mess it up, and you have too much hair for me to avoid that. In fact, strip the shirt off too. I'm doing this style in the buff."

This wasn't new. Sabastian was known for talking guys into taking off their shirts before getting styled. This was the first time he'd asked me, though. I'd been working on the farm, so I knew I'd developed a bit more muscle than I'd had when I lived in New York.

I gave him a sour look and he smiled back at me innocently.

Then in his flippant way, he said, "Well, if I had a body like that, I'd never put a shirt on."

"Whatever," I said and laughed as I handed Eddie the shirt and jacket.

When he was done, I had a conservative yet stylish cut. Not as wild as the first style he'd given me, thank God. You never knew with Sabastian what kind of style you were getting. Eddie must have let him know I was going to be coming in and where I was going that night.

Once we were done, I was coiffed for the night. Eddie hesitantly gave my clothes back, saying I actually looked better without the tux. But I refused to walk down the street without clothes on.

"Who are you taking to this party?" Sabastian asked as I got dressed again.

I smiled. "My publisher, of course."

They frowned. "Who?" Eddie asked. "Some old publisher?"

"Oh, you probably don't know him. I think he's pretty solitary."

"Try us," Sabastian said, hands on his hips.

"Liam Rickard," I said as I looked into the mirror, playing with a loose strand of hair.

Sabastian slapped my hand and told me not to mess with perfection. Then he and Eddie stared at me with shocked looks on their faces.

"What?" I asked.

"You're going to *the* Tiffany Rickard's Save the Ocean gala with her son, Liam Rickard?" Eddie asked and both he and Sabastian continued to stare at me with their mouths agape.

"Seriously, how do you both know where I'm going?" I asked. "Did I accidentally let it slip?"

"Bitch, please," Eddie said. "I already told you, we know every social event in this city. Tiffany Rickard's gala is a huge deal. I'm still not sure how you got an invite. Not that you have a clue what that means."

He sighed and slipped down into Sabastian's chair. Sabastian automatically began running his fingers through Eddie's hair, looking for imperfections as he shot me furtive glances.

"Okay, so spit it out. What's wrong with Liam Rickard?" I asked.

Eddie turned the chair to look at me. "Nothing is *wrong* with Liam Rickard. He's just New York's most eligible bachelor and basically refuses to go out after his last..."

Eddie hesitated and I gave him my *you better spit it out* look.

Sabastian took over.

"Liam had a horrible breakup about five years ago. He dated his father's attorney, a man almost twice his age. The guy messed him up really bad, and as far as anyone knows he's not dated anyone since. Well, at least not until tonight."

"So, you're telling me I'm going to be the first guy he's been out with in public for five years? And that's going to be some sort of big deal?" I asked.

They both nodded in unison. If the information they were giving me wasn't so scary and intense, I'd have laughed at their matching expressions.

"Well, fuck me!" I said and fell onto the stool Sabastian kept next to his station.

"Has he already done that?" Sabastian asked with a chuckle.

I shook my head, lying. I'd go to my grave with that information. Sabastian and Eddie were my stylish friends, and although I thought them a bit shallow, they'd always been good friends. Despite that, I knew that whatever I told them would become the talk of the town. They were both notorious gossips, and I didn't want to cheapen what Liam and I had. Nor did I want to be his bounce-back after his five-year dry spell.

"Well, maybe that'll change once he gets a look at you in that," Sabastian said. "You really do look stunning. My styling, of course, is the cream on the head!"

"You two were made for each other," I said, and they both blushed. "Shit, no! You finally hooked up?"

"Well, look at the time," Sabastian said and began shooing us out. "I have other clients, you know, so you better go."

"Oh no!" I exclaimed, turning back around. "You better spit it out. How long has this been going on?"

"You can't tell anyone," Eddie said. "We don't want it getting around."

"Well, not yet," Sabastian whispered. "We're just enjoying letting it be between us."

I smiled. "Well, I can't say I'm surprised. The two of you have been moony-eyed over each other for years."

"Moony-eyed? Damn, you're still such a hick," Eddie said, but I could tell he was trying to divert the conversation.

I reached over and kissed his cheek, then did the same for Sabastian.

"I'm so happy for you both, and I want to be the maid of honor when you get married!"

"Fuck you," Eddie said, and both Sabastian and I laughed.

"The forever bachelor is having a difficult time with this, I see."

Eddie just gave me a withering look.

I put my arm into his and led him out of the salon.

"See ya, Sabastian," I said while he laughed behind me.

As we walked back toward Eddie's apartment, he leaned into me.

"I like him so much, but I'm afraid I'm going to fuck it all up," he confided.

"Why? How would you fuck it up?" I asked.

"'Cause I'm a damned snob, and he's so real and, and well, he's so put together. He's refused my advances for years, and now that I've finally convinced him to give me a chance, I'm scared that I'll do or say something wrong."

I chuckled and put my arm around Eddie's shoulder.

"Honey, he really is moony-eyed over you. Listen, he probably knows you better than anyone in this town. If he's finally giving you a chance, I doubt you'll fuck it up. Unless you cheat on him or something."

Eddie looked shy.

"Well, he said he wants to keep it open."

"Bullshit," I replied. "Sabastian is not an open relationship sort of guy. You screw around and you'll definitely lose him. I'll tell you right now, *that* is a test!"

Eddie sighed. "I thought so, too. But why would he be testing me? I'd rather just be up-front about it. If he wants a monogamous relationship with me, why wouldn't he just come out and say that?"

I narrowed my eyes at him. "Because you're a slut. I've known you for years and every week it seems like you have a new man on your arm. Hell, you fuck around more than my ex did. I'm guessing he wants to know that you want him enough to be exclusive. He's putting the ball in your court."

Eddie sighed again, this time more deeply. "I've never felt like this about anyone else but being in a monogamous relationship scares me. Like I'm going to fuck it up."

"Do you want to fuck other people?" I asked.

"Well, not right now. Sabastian fills me up," he said, and I laughed naughtily.

"Not that way." He pushed me away, then said, "Well, okay, that way, too. But you know what I mean, he touches my insides...fuck it, I give up."

I pulled Eddie back into me and gave him a huge smooch on the cheek.

"I've never seen the great Eddie Monroe this worked up over a guy before. I get it, you like him a lot. So, it sounds to me like you'd better make some fast decisions. Can you give up your lifestyle and make him your number one? Sabastian isn't a player and has no tolerance for them. You'll have to profess your undying love for him and pepper him with love and attention the rest of your life if you want to keep him. But, of course, you already know that."

When we got back to Eddie's apartment, I gathered my things and promised to get the tux and shoes back to him unharmed.

I thought about Liam as I rode in the taxi back to my hotel. He and I had spent the past few nights together, laughing and getting to know each other. The more time I spent with him, the more I liked him. Most of my preconceived notions about Liam Rickard appeared to be wrong. Still pretentious and clearly born with a silver spoon in his mouth, he was different than other men who'd grown up like that, more put together, and a little less naïve about the world around him. I attributed that to Tiffany, of course. She had a pretty significant silver spoon as well, but at least she didn't mind getting her hands dirty, and she cared about more than what the next fashion was or when the next gala event would be.

Liam had agreed to pick me up and drive me over to his parents' place for the gala. I had barely enough time after the cab dropped me off to grab a bite to eat. These galas always had crappy finger food and tons of people looking over your shoulder judging what and how much you ate. I'd discovered after my first gala with Randy to eat first so you could just sip champagne until you were able to extricate yourself from the event.

I was brushing my teeth when Liam knocked on my door. I finished brushing, checked myself in the mirror one last time, and thanked the Universe that I had stylish friends who could clean me up and make me presentable.

When I pulled the door open, Liam's eye grew wide.

"Fuck," he said and pushed me back into the room. "Mom can screw the gala. Let's stay here."

I laughed. "Shut up, I promised your mom."

Liam was kissing my neck just above the collar of my shirt and I was considering letting his mom down when he finally stepped back.

"God, you look so..."

"So unlike me?" I asked.

"No, it's you. But let's just say you clean up really, *really* well!"

I chuckled.

"Okay, come on before I get a hard-on and can't walk," he said with a mischievous smile as he grabbed my arm.

When we got into his car, I looked over at him.

"Liam?" I asked, and he turned toward me, smiling. "Am I the first person you've been out with in public in five years?"

He hesitated. "Yeah. How did you know?"

"Let's just say the people who styled me to look like this are busybodies."

He put his hands on the wheel and sighed. "Yeah, I had a bad breakup. It did bad things to my insides and I didn't really want to date anyone. Hookups took care of my sexual needs, and well, then I inherited my dad's job at the company. Five years just went by fast."

I sighed too and leaned back into the posh upholstery. "Isn't this going to be opening a can of worms?" I asked.

"Maybe, but the rumor mill doesn't really make much difference in the grand scheme of things. Our company publishes your books. You are about to release your next book tomorrow, so unless you jump my bones tonight, the New York grapevine will probably just assume I'm bringing you because of that."

I *hmphed.* "You and I both know better than that. They'll be planning our wedding and making a huge stink about it the moment we walk through that door."

He glanced over at me and smiled. "You're probably right, but who cares? Even if we weren't fucking like rabbits, I'd want you on my arm. You're quite a looker, for a pig farmer."

I reached over and pinched him through his tux, and he leaned over to kiss me.

"Let's go rock the New York scene, shall we?"

"Sure. But I wanna leave as soon as possible. Seriously, I'd rather not be there long."

"Agreed," he said.

Liam Rickard

Bobby Devereaux was the most handsome man I knew. He didn't usually play up his features, but when he did, it was devastating. The fact that he didn't know how handsome he was made him both perplexing and, strangely, more appealing.

He shocked me when he mentioned the five-year stretch. Since he hadn't brought it up before, I'd figured he was so out of the New York social scene that he didn't know, or maybe he just didn't care. When he did bring it up, it threw me, and I wasn't sure how to navigate the situation.

My ex, Atticus Sterling, had been a friend of my father's. Hell, for all I know, he might still be a friend of his. I'd fallen for him in a stupid and ridiculous way that could only be attributed to inexperience and youth. My father had been angry at me when he'd found out about us. It was almost like he was jealous. We lasted just under a year, and the entire time, my father barely spoke to me.

When I caught Atticus in bed with two other guys, having a three-way in the bed we shared, he'd laughed at me for being upset.

"Be a man, not a pussy!" he'd yelled as I stormed out.

Luckily, I hadn't seen the fucker since then. Still, the betrayal had stabbed me in the heart and made me cynical, uninterested in pursuing another serious relationship.

I'd known that bringing Bobby would cause a stir at the gala, but Mom had invited him. And I wanted to be with him, so I figured as long as he didn't stick his tongue down my throat, we could just play it off as professional.

Knowing him, though, the sweet, unconscious way he touched me would quickly alert the world to the fact that there was more going on than a professional relationship. I'd thought about that a lot over the past few days, but what I'd finally figured out was that I didn't give a fuck what people thought. I liked him a lot and more than I'd liked anyone in a very long time. If he was going to my mom's gala, he sure as hell was going as *my date*, especially now I'd seen him dressed up like a supermodel.

When we walked in, eyes turned our way. It wasn't unusual. These galas were as much about being seen as they were about whatever charity they were sponsoring. But the wide eyes following us, and the whispered gossip, were unusual.

To Bobby's credit, he pretended not to notice. When my mom saw him, she pulled him into a huge hug.

"You look amazing!" she whispered in his ear. Then she looked at me, winking.

Mom could still make me blush like a teenager caught looking at porn, but despite my embarrassment, I was thrilled that she approved of him. Why was it that, even at twenty-nine years old, I still wanted her approval?

She pulled Bobby around to meet the people she considered her actual friends, whom I knew were very few and far between. The handful of people was *her* crowd. I'd known most of them all my life and knew them to be fierce activists for various causes, just like my mother. Before long, Bobby was genuinely enjoying himself. Laughing with Mom's friends, he was passed around to everyone she knew he would relate to and he was deliberately kept away from the more egotistical crowd.

It was hard to keep up with them, and eventually, I gave up trying. My dad came up behind me in the kitchen when I ducked in there to catch my breath. The gossipy chit-chat was making my head hurt.

"He's quite the looker," my dad said, causing me to smile.

"You think?" I replied.

My dad just *hmphed.* "His first book is doing well. Do you think book two will also?"

"There sure is every indication that it will. He started book three this week. Been working on it since he's been here. He won't let me read it yet, though."

Dad nodded. "Authors are peculiar people. Best to let him have his space while he's creating."

I smiled. My father had been CEO of Rickard Publishing for twenty-three years before retiring and handing the reins to me. I figured if anyone knew the peculiarities of authors, it would be him.

We sat in comfortable silence, nibbling on trays of party food and avoiding the crowd. He and I still had difficulty relating to one another, but we were getting better.

"You aren't going to chastise me for dating an author we work with?" I finally asked.

He chuckled. "No, I've decided not to get involved with your sex life any longer. Besides, he's a looker, like I said. And he's popular with all your mom's friends, which says a lot about his character. Your mom likes him, too. That says he's more than just what meets the eye."

I nodded. "Well, I guess I'd better get back out there. I'm going to try to pry him away from all of this soon."

"Why don't you bring him by for Sunday brunch? I'm sure your mom would enjoy seeing him, and he can help us get rid of all this wretched food!"

I laughed out loud. My father hated the finger foods from these galas and Mom always bought too much just to be sure not to run out. Since she refused to waste food, she'd force us to eat it at every meal until it was gone.

When I walked back into the main room, I didn't see Bobby. I wandered around until I spotted my mother, who looked alarmed. I followed her line of sight and, seeing Bobby cornered by his ex and the guy that had split them up, I quickly made my way over to him.

When I got to him, I leaned in and kissed his neck.

"There you are, honey. Are you about ready to leave?" I whispered in his ear.

He smiled and looked at me.

"Well, in a moment. What's your hurry?" he asked.

I looked up at him in surprise, and he had a mischievous grin on his face.

"Sweetheart," he said, letting a light country twang slip into his voice, which he only did when he was intentionally trying to make a point. "This is Randy Fletcher and...well, I'm sorry, I don't remember your name."

I noticed both men squint at the slight.

"We know each other already," Randy said.

I smiled and said, "Yes, Randy. Nice to see you too, Jessie."

Bobby turned to me. "Jessie. Yes, that's right. Although we really never officially met until tonight. We've only talked to one another over...*Facebook*."

He emphasized the name of the website.

I smothered a smile. My mom had filled me in on the rumors regarding what had gone down. Jessie—when he'd been on the outs with Randy—had told everyone the truth about what had happened. Since then, Jessie and Randy had dated off and on but seemed to be somewhat incompatible.

"I'm sorry to pull him away, but tomorrow is going to be a huge day. You know, he's releasing his second book at Comic-Con. He is so adored there, I'm sure the crowds will be driving him insane." I noticed we had quite an audience, so I kept up the show. "Hon, don't you think you should get back, so you're well-rested for tomorrow's big reveal?"

"Well," he looked at his watch. "We probably still have time for *extracurricular* activities." He emphasized the word in a suggestive manner, then said, "But yes, darling, we probably do need to go. Randy, Jessie, a pleasure as always."

He shook both men's hands like they were old acquaintances and then allowed me to escort him toward my mom. She hugged us both and winked before sending us on our way.

As soon as we were in the elevator, he leaned into me and sighed. "I didn't know those things could be fun. I like your mom's friends."

"Yeah, they liked you, too. Which is odd because they don't usually like anyone," I said blushing.

He put his hand over mine as I drove him back to his hotel. I was looking forward to getting him out of that tux for those *extracurricular* activities he'd mentioned earlier.

"Randy seemed upset," I said sarcastically.

He shrugged. "I doubt it. We weren't really all that close. He was just telling me all about how he and Jessie...that's his name, right?" he asked.

When I nodded, he continued. "I guess he and Jessie have moved in together and they hired someone to renovate the place. Maybe he wanted it more pretentious...whatever."

He laid his head back on the headrest.

"You really are over him, aren't you?" I asked, curious.

He looked over at me without lifting his head. "Like, from the moment I finished writing the first book."

I looked at him and, thinking out loud, said, "You really use writing as a way to express yourself, don't you?"

He lifted his head off the seat this time, thinking, then nodded. "Yeah, I suppose I do. It's a form of therapy, I guess."

I squeezed his knee affectionately.

"It's cool," I replied. "It's like an artist expressing him or herself on the canvas."

"That's sort of how I think of it myself," he admitted.

"Do you ever just write for fun?" I asked.

"Is CEO Liam asking, or boyfriend Liam?"

I thought for a moment. "Boyfriend," I replied.

"Yes, I have a journal. I've always kept one since Mrs. McMillian, my third-grade teacher, forced us to start writing in them for part of our grade."

"Can I read them?" I asked, and he laughed.

"My third-grade journals?" he asked, laughing. "No, you can't read my journals. They're private, of course, and I tend to burn them after I'm done writing, anyway. My siblings were nosy, so I learned early on to get rid of any writing that could come back to bite me."

I sighed. "That's too bad. I'd like to have seen what Mr. Bobby Devereaux had to say about meeting a certain publisher."

Bobby laughed out loud. "Those have definitely been destroyed!"

"What did you write about me?" I asked, letting my hand slowly rub up and down his thigh.

"I think you already know," he said. "Now, stop poking and get back to the hotel. I'd like to have my way with a *certain publisher*."

Since our first sexplosion, the sex had become much gentler and sweeter. Maybe because we had been fucking every night that week and we hadn't gone long enough between sessions to give our libidos enough time to *need* to explode.

We stripped and got into bed. Bobby straddled me grinding his cock into mine before he bent over to take my cock into his mouth. He stared into my eyes as he dragged his tongue up and down my shaft.

I loved watching him as he sucked me. Something about it made my heart quake.

Not wanting to risk coming too soon, I pulled Bobby up over my body, our cocks rubbing against each other as he slowly slid up to meet my mouth in a tangle of tongues. I rolled him over, still kissing him, still grinding our cocks together. The tantalizing friction drew a long moan from him as it always did when we frotted.

"I want you to fuck me," I whispered against his mouth. He pulled his head back and looked at me, brow furrowed questioningly. Until now, I'd always topped.

He must have seen my desire for him because the surprised look turned to a naughty smile.

"You think you can handle this?" he said, and I knew he meant his cock.

Bobby's cock wasn't longer than average, but it was almost obscenely thick. To be honest, its girth had intimidated me from the beginning, but that didn't stop me from wondering what it would feel like to have him inside me, stretching and filling my hole.

"Well, not without a little help," I said, getting up and walking over to my overnight bag.

I reached in and pulled out a vibrator dildo.

"I don't usually bottom. Hell, I've only let one guy top me, and it required some work. You still up for it?" I asked, feeling shy.

Bobby's smile widened, and he looked positively wicked as he got up.

He tugged the cock-shaped vibrator from my grasp and pressed me back onto the bed, nipping at my lower lip and pulling on it with his teeth as he rutted against me, our cocks, now slick with pre-cum, sliding against each other until I was aching with need.

He kissed along my jaw until his mouth was against my ear and whispered, "This is gonna be fun."

I shuddered, both at the words themselves and the vibration of his words against my ear.

Bobby pulled the bottle of lube out of the side table. We'd bought it when we realized small portable packets weren't going to be adequate for the amount of sex we were having.

He slowly lubed up the vibrator and turned it on before lifting my right leg. He maintained eye contact as he began to tease my hole with it, moving it across the sensitive pucker and forcing the muscles to relax.

The rigid vibrator contrasted intensely with the warmth of Bobby's mouth as he leaned over, taking my cock, blowing me as he navigated the vibrator into place.

He looked at me for direction as he began to penetrate me. I immediately tensed and when he pulled back I took the dildo from him and began to slowly fuck myself with it.

His smile returned and he went back to sucking me.

"Bring your cock up here," I said, wanting to suck him as I fucked myself.

Bobby's naughty smile returned to his face as he moved his cock to my mouth gently teasing me with it. I reached around him and stabilized him with my empty hand.

Bobby took the dildo back from me before straddling my head fucking my mouth, then lifting my legs so I could fuck myself more easily with the vibrator.

He moved his fingers next to the dildo and massaged as it worked its magic.

When he added a finger to my hole beside the vibrator, I thought I would come right then. I'd always been vocal. Having my hole penetrated by both his finger and the vibrator was so intense, so wonderful. When he began to thrust his cock deep into my throat, the ecstasy was almost more than I could handle.

I pulled my mouth off his cock to moan at the sensation. The moan turned into a shout as he tormented my ass with the toy. "Fuck! Bobby, fuck me! Oh, fuckkk...that feels..."

He cut off my wails by thrusting his cock back between my lips into my throat, and my entire body shivered, overwhelmed at being impaled at both ends. It was too much, yet not enough.

Bobby must have thought so, too. He pulled away, reached for the extra-large condom, and quickly rolled it over his obscenely swollen cock.

"Think you're ready?" He gently slid the vibrator out of my well-stretched hole, switching it off and tossing it across the bed.

The sight of this hunk of a man straddling me, stroking his sheathed cock with lube, was enough to undo me.

"You need to fuck me now!" I growled, reaching for him as if to hurry him along. I wanted, no, needed, to feel him inside me, and I needed him to know it. I needed him to know that if he didn't fuck me soon, I was going to come all over myself.

A knowing grin spread across his face as his eyes met mine, saw my desperation. He nudged the head of his cock against my waiting hole.

I arched, enjoying the contrast between him and the hard plastic of the dildo.

"Bobby..." I murmured, unable to think, much less talk.

He guided his cock into me carefully, his girth stretching that ring of muscle until it burned, but as the sting turned to pleasure I found myself pushing back against him, chasing Bobby's cock as he began to pump harder and deeper into me.

I don't think I'd ever wanted someone this much.

"Fuck," I kept chanting. "Fuck, fuck..."

Bobby Devereaux

Being inside Liam was unraveling me. I knew it wouldn't take much for me to come. Just seeing this powerful man lying there. Taking me. Wanting me.

"Liam, you're so hot, so tight!" I moaned as he pushed back against my cock, driving it deeper into his hole.

"Mmm..." he hummed, my girth stretching him as he impaled himself on me until my balls rested against his ass.

He lay still then, not breathing, and I knew he was trying to get used to me being there.

I could feel the moment it switched from painful to...more.

I pulled back and then thrust back in. He drew in a deep breath, sighing.

"Bobby, please..."

He'd never begged me. In fact, he'd always been in control, even when I was sucking him. The vulnerability caused my brain to short-circuit. I thrust into him repeatedly as he writhed with pleasure beneath me.

I began to let the sensation take me.

He moaned louder and louder as I increased my rhythm.

"Fuck, Bobby! Fuck!"

When he began to match my movements with his, I increased my speed.

Liam reached for me, his hungry mouth locking mine into the kiss to end all kisses.

He released my mouth only to squeeze my cock with his tight passage. "Fuck. Me. Hard." He rocked his hips to punctuate each word.

I shoved my cock into him, and he reared up in ecstasy.

"Fuck me!" he yelled, and I happily complied.

The sweat rolled off both of us and I took him harder and harder until I must have hit his prostate because his eyes opened in shock and his mouth formed a perfect 0.

His eyes fluttered shut again as I rocked into that sweet spot, knowing the effect it was having on him, pegging it repeatedly to drive him out of his mind. I watched as he gave himself over to the pleasure before exploding, shooting his load all over his stomach and chest.

Watching him, feeling the pure heated pleasure he

radiated, sent me crashing over the edge and only seconds later I emptied into the condom

I fell next to him and rolled into his arms. I almost, *almost* told him I loved him in the heat of the moment. But as I lay there, I thanked the Universe that I'd gotten my head straight before I did.

I disposed of the condom and put the vibrator in the bathroom to be cleaned later before I came back and tenderly wiped Liam off with a warm washcloth.

Liam watched me with sleepy satisfied eyes causing my heart to do a funny little flutter before I tossed the cloth into the bathroom and climbed back into the bed next to him. Neither of us spoke but rather fell into a deep sleep cuddled into one another.

***

My book reveal was late the next morning. I'd intentionally avoided the Comic-Con events prior to my release date to keep from having to answer any questions about the new book before it was time. The event was held at Madison Square Garden, and it was absolutely packed.

I'm sure that made Liam happy. Once we'd gone our separate ways that morning, I hadn't seen hide nor hair of the man. Doug ended up taking me out to breakfast, and when I clued him in to the fact that I was dating Liam, he shook his head.

"Not really something your agent wants to hear, but I guess it was inevitable. The two of you are like teenagers when you're around one another."

I told him I'd started a new book, and his eyes lit up before his face dropped.

"Does Liam already know?"

"Well, yeah. I did mention we are dating."

Doug sighed a long-suffering sigh. "Why do you even need an agent when you've got the damned publisher in your bed?"

I raised my eyebrows at him and laughed. "Ah, honey, you're my first love. Don't you ever forget that!"

Doug looked at me and shook his head, "Don't try to manipulate me with those pretty eyes, young man."

I laughed. "At least I'm writing a third book," I said. "Isn't that something to celebrate?"

"If you insist," he said to me as he looked around to find a server, then yelled out for her to bring us two mimosas.

"I wasn't going to tell anyone. I sort of let it slip to Liam. If this book isn't received well, the next sure won't be. If I'm going to be a fiction writer, which you know I never intended to be, then I need to make sure my writing is making a difference. I don't want to just write fluff pieces."

"We'll know soon enough." Doug shrugged.

I smiled, the excitement coursing through me.

"I'm so nervous," I admitted. "I've never felt this vulnerable before. Everyone will be judging my work, looking for every flaw."

"Well, that's exactly what they're doing. But this book is awesome. Different, and a bit more intense than the last, but no more so than Marvel tends to be."

I nodded, pondering how much I wanted to reveal.

"Well, if this one is successful, then I have at least three others in my mind. If it's not, I'm going back to my plan of going into journalism."

Doug nodded. "Or, you could look at a non-fiction piece."

"Or...there's lots of *ors*, but let's just keep our fingers crossed about this avenue."

The reveal was awesome. I didn't actually have much to do with it since Liam's company did the intro and brought me on stage. I just read a few of the more intense passages, then I was stuck on a stage, signing books. My hand was cramping by the time they shut the line down.

"I swear I signed ten thousand books," I said as Doug came to get me.

"It was a lot, and it could've been a lot more. Next time, we need to plan ahead and have you sign them before the reveal."

"I agree! God help me, I totally agree."

I let Doug know I was headed back to the hotel to take a quick nap. Of course, I didn't tell him I needed the nap because Liam and I had been up late into the night making love.

The hotel was only a few blocks from Comic-Con, so after saying goodbye to Doug, I walked back to the hotel and up to my room only to collapse on the bed for a nice nap. When I woke up, Liam was tucked up next to me. As I stretched and yawned, he nuzzled closer, holding me tight.

I laughed and moaned. "This is a nice surprise. How did you get in?"

"I told the front desk I forgot my key," he said sleepily.

"How did they know you were with me?"

"I think since I've spent the night here every night this week. They were pretty sure we were together."

"Mmm." I stretched again, enjoying how his body felt next to mine. "I guess that's true. Got everything taken down at Comic-Con?"

He nodded. "Yeah, it's good to be the boss. I could just leave and let them handle it all."

I smiled. "That's true. It felt pretty good to be the author as well. Grunt workers are the best, you should give them all a raise!"

"I'm not sure the board would agree with you. Or the stockholders."

"That's too bad," I said as I turned over so the two of us could snuggle more easily.

"I told my friend Eddie I'd have the tux back to him. I need to do that, or he'll send the fashion police after me."

"Let's do it tomorrow. I have a surprise for you tonight."

"Really?" I asked, feeling excited.

"Yep, in two hours. Are you hungry? I called to see if you wanted to go out, but when you didn't answer, I came to get you. You looked so peaceful, I decided to join you instead."

"You made the right choice. What's the surprise?"

"Can't say, then it wouldn't be a surprise."

I climbed on top of him and began kissing his face.

"Please, please, tell me," I begged. He laughed at my frustration until I started tickling him, then he flipped and pinned me under him to end the onslaught.

"You'll like it, I promise. Just trust me."

I was growing hard while he lay on top of me. "I kinda like this!"

He ground into me for a minute, then stopped. "Later. Now, go get ready."

He crawled off me and I jumped into the shower to wash my hair. The nap had given me a serious case of bedhead.

As I was drying off, I yelled into the room, "What do I need to wear?"

"You can wear what you had on today if you want or dress up. Either way, it's business casual."

"So, no t-shirt?"

"Preferably not, but if that's all you brought with you..."

"Besides the tux, I have a button-down and a pair of new dark jeans. That's the best I can do."

He came in and pulled my naked body up against him.

"That'll be perfect."

He began to kiss my neck, the way he always did that made me horny as hell.

"If you want me to get ready, you'll have to stop that, like, right now. Otherwise, I'm stripping you and tossing you on the bed."

"Mmm, that sounds great." He pulled off quickly, though. "But this sounds great too."

We dressed, and when he asked what sounded good to eat, I chose Mexican without even thinking about it. Before I knew it, we were at Los Tacos on 43rd Street.

I'd eaten there before and always enjoyed the food. The chicken Asada was my favorite, but I mostly filled up with chips and salsa.

I was in a great mood as we walked out of the restaurant and down the road toward 44th Street. When we came to the theater where *Gerls*, a crazy popular musical starring the amazing Suzie Fisher, was playing, I looked at Liam in surprise. "You got us tickets to see *Gerls* with Beta?"

He laughed. "Are you going to geek out on me?"

I nodded, eyes wide. "I'm totally gonna geek out on you!"

"Good, cause yep." He pulled out two tickets.

I did a little dance in the street. "I almost bought tickets for myself but didn't know what was going on this week. I'm so excited! I've been dying to see this in person. Suzie Fisher is so fucking hot!"

"Oh, you're way behind the times," Liam said. "It's Suzie Freemont now."

"I did hear that. She just got married, didn't she?"

"About a year ago, now."

I sighed and leaned into Liam as we stood in line. I loved the theater. Not that I went much when I'd lived here. Randy had thought the theater was stupid, so he'd never wanted to go, and I couldn't afford to go often with my low salary from the paper. So, mostly I had to content myself with a few of the lower-priced shows. Not that I didn't love those, sometimes more than the big productions, but *Gerls* was so awesome and had already won numerous awards. The thing that really sent me spinning was a recent press release stating that Suzie Freemont had announced this was her last year on the show. I wanted to see it before she left.

"You know, I almost met her in person," I said as we came up to the theater.

"Really?" Liam asked, genuinely interested.

"Yeah, when I first got to New York, my coworkers dragged me to a gay bar. She came in and the entire place started chanting, "Beta! Beta!" It was epic."

"So, why didn't you meet her?" he asked.

"Well, my life took a distinctly different path...that's the exact moment I met Randy."

Liam pulled me around and looked at me seriously.

"Are you sure this is okay, then?" he asked.

I grinned ear to ear. "Dude, this is a dream come true," and kissed him with as much seduction as I could muster while standing in a long line of onlookers.

I shouldn't have been surprised when we were seated in the best seats in the house, right in the orchestra section. I try not to be a snob and would've been happy in the cheap seats, but, oh, my God! I was about to see Suzie Freemont perform as Beta in the musical *Gerls and* I was in the good seats.

Suzie owned the stage like a goddess. When she sang her lament to Lydia, I cried like a baby. The song had earned notoriety outside of the musical theater community, and my favorite music app station played it all the time. Seeing it in its context was both magical and gut-wrenching.

Liam pulled a package of tissues from his coat pocket and handed one to me.

"I'm a geek," I whispered, embarrassed. But I noticed I wasn't the only one crying, so I didn't feel quite so bad.

When the production was over, I was emotionally exhausted. I'd laughed and cried and had to resist singing every song with the cast. It truly was one of the best productions around, and with all the vampires and zombies and monsters, it was like the audience had somehow been transported into this gothic Victorian mixed-up steampunk world.

As the lights came up, I looked over at Liam, who was watching me with interest. I laid a huge kiss on him, right on the lips.

"That was the best surprise ever!" I exclaimed, and several people looked over at us.

I couldn't have cared less. I'd just seen *Gerls* while on the arm of a sexy-as-fuck man. I'd released my second book that day, and I was as happy as a man could be. Life could end right then, and I'd be satisfied.

I was getting ready to leave, but Liam said, "Let everyone else go. There's another part to the surprise."

I sat back down, uncomfortable that we were the only people still sitting. Once most of the people were gone, however, he stood and pulled me up next to him. We followed the last of the people out, but instead of leaving the building, he led me through a nondescript door that opened onto a long, dark hallway.

"What's this?" I asked.

"You'll see," he said, and even though it was dark, I could tell he was smiling.

When we reached a rustic part of the theater, where I assumed concessions were brought in from the back alley, I was pulled down another hallway and up a set of stairs. I could hear the activity before we got to it, and I was beginning to suspect what was about to happen.

At the top of the stairs, there was a swarm of activity. The crew was bouncing around, putting things away, laughing and cutting up with the supporting members of the cast. Just being backstage was exciting enough, but when Liam grabbed my hand and pulled me through the crowd of people, I almost peed myself. Suzie herself stepped up to Liam and shook his hand.

"Hi, Suzie. This is Bobby Devereaux. Your agent said you wanted to meet him."

Suzie squealed and jumped up and down. I wondered how anyone could do a two-and-a-half-hour performance and still have the energy to jump up and down.

The next thing I knew, I was in a sweaty bear hug and she was asking me several questions about my characters and the book that had just been released.

Liam pulled a copy of my book out of his jacket, and I wondered how the hell he'd stored it there without me knowing. He handed it to me, along with a pen, and asked if I wanted to use his back to sign it for her.

I stood, mouth agape, unable to process the world I'd just been thrust into.

Suzie apologized. "Did I overwhelm you? I do that to people. Sorry."

"No," I managed to get out. "I'm just a geeky fan of yours, and Liam didn't warn me that I was coming back here to meet you and he sure didn't tell me I was here to sign a book for you."

We both looked at Liam, and I said, "Liam is an asshole." That caused Suzie to laugh out loud.

A tall, stocky man came up behind her then and put his arm around her.

"I see you met Mr. Devereaux," he said, and she turned to him and kissed him full on the mouth.

"We are having a mutual geek-out, so give us a moment," she said, and I laughed.

"Bobby, this is my husband, Indi Freemont. Indi, this is Bobby Devereaux, author of the best books ever written!"

I smiled at Indi, then looked back at Suzie. "I'll answer all your questions if you answer mine!"

She laughed and pulled me into another hug.

I signed the book, Your greatest geeky friend, Bobby Devereaux, and handed it to her.

She squealed again and, after doing a little happy dance, she said, "If you two don't have plans, I'm meeting my brother and his husband, as well as Indy's brother and husband at our favorite dive. If you can join us, I'm sure they'd be thrilled!"

"Yes," I replied and then looked at Liam. "Sorry I answered for you, but fuck, you can go back to the hotel. I'm going with them."

Liam laughed. "I see where I rank, but I'd love to join you as well."

Liam Rickard

It was fun to watch Bobby geek out over the show. Indigo Freemont, Suzie's husband and agent, had contacted our company to see if Bobby would be willing to come to the show and meet her afterward.

Apparently, Suzie was a big Bobby Devereaux fan and was planning to skip out on that night's show just to come to Comic-Con to see him. Indigo had to intervene somehow. The only way they could stop her from taking off was to promise that Bobby would be at the show.

I figured Roy had known Bobby the longest, so I'd asked him what he thought. He'd told us how big a Broadway fan Bobby was, so I decided it would be worth the risk of making this a surprise.

We arrived at the total dive of a restaurant Suzie insisted on. It looked more like a high-school kid hangout than somewhere an award-winning Broadway star would eat. We were immediately greeted by a crowd. I recognized Suzie's brother, Aiden Fisher, and geeked out a little myself. My parents had once bid on one of his art pieces but had been outbid by the Louvre. They had ended up buying one of his New York pieces instead, although we all knew the Louvre collection was his best work. I'd obsessively followed his work ever since.

Of course, I'd known Suzie and Aiden were siblings, but I hadn't expected him to be there that night.

Across from him, another equally famous couple sat grinning from ear to ear. Clay Masters and Denim Freemont, two supermodels who had become New York's most beloved duo after posing together in a designer jean ad that had become an international sensation.

I had to admit, although I was less intrigued by them than I was by Aiden, the sight of the two men turned me on. Not just because they both had beautiful bodies, which they most certainly did, but because of how the two looked at one another. As I watched them, I couldn't help glancing over at Bobby and thinking that's what my expression must look like when I looked at him.

When the press had gotten wind that Denim had proposed to Clay just before their famous shot was taken, the electricity had sparked all over the world and the ad spent months floating across social media.

All six people fawned over Bobby. There were well-read copies of his first novel strewn across the table, and when Aiden shyly produced a Sharpie, Bobby giggled and began signing them. Suzie ordered milkshakes of various flavors for everyone. When the shakes arrived, everyone let Bobby choose first.

We talked about all kinds of topics, but once it came out that Bobby still actively worked on his family's farm in Iowa, everyone was curious about what that was like. Until that information came out, Aiden's husband Devin hadn't spoken three words. But as soon as the two started talking shop, Devin was as inquisitive as the rest. The quiet, brooding and massively attractive cattle-rancher convinced Bobby that he needed to come to their ranch in Washington and spend some time with him and Aiden.

We talked until the restaurant's sole server kicked us out. The group begged us to go out with them for brunch the next day, but we had to decline because of my dad's invitation. Truthfully, I would much rather hang out with this rag-tag bunch of people who were significantly more fun to spend time with than my parents.

When we got back to the hotel room, Bobby and I both stripped and collapsed into each other's arms, too tired and happy to do anything but fall asleep.

I woke up at my regular time and had to force myself to stay in bed so I could get a few more hours sleep. Finally, by nine, I couldn't stay in bed any longer, so I slipped out of Bobby's arms and into the shower. When I came out, Bobby was still dead to the world, so I went into the living room and opened my computer to see the reviews.

They were good, but it was still early. The critics said Bobby's new style took some getting used to, and some even said it was like the story had been written by a different author altogether, which wasn't surprising. I think the critics were waiting to see what the social media reaction would be.

Finally, Bobby came out of the bedroom and collapsed next to me on the little sofa. He laid his head on my shoulder.

"Good reviews?" he asked.

"Good enough."

Bobby smiled. "When do you think they'll start rolling in?" he asked.

"Probably middle of next week. The public will begin putting out initial reviews like the ones here, but this is not the time to worry about reviews. We have all those fancy leftovers from the party waiting at my parent's house. We need to go finish them off before my Dad starts to panic."

***

Brunch at my parents' house was interesting. My father was his usual standoffish self. I could tell he was critical of Bobby, but I guessed that was because of some residual stuff from our conflict over my affair with Atticus.

Mom, however, was crazy about Bobby, and my dad's cool manner didn't seem to make a difference during brunch.

When Mom pulled Bobby into a room to show him my baby pictures, I hung back and asked Dad, "So, what's wrong? I thought you wanted us to come over?"

Dad shook his head. "It's just that I heard some things after you left the party, things about him being a social climber and looking for a free ride."

"Yeah, you heard this from his ex?" I asked.

Dad shook his head. "Well, that's where it originated. But no, I heard it from Atticus," he said.

Hearing my dad say the man's name for the first time in five years shocked me into silence.

I stared at the rug for a few moments before I asked, "How would Atticus even know him?"

Dad shrugged. "He seems to be an expert on the matter."

"Well, until you find out how he knows all this, I would caution you to reserve judgment."

I stood up and walked back to where Mom and Bobby were pouring over baby pictures. My father had really upset me not just because he was still associating with that horrible man—despite knowing what he'd done to me—but also because he believed what was clearly slander instead of considering the evidence in front of him.

I shook it off. This wasn't the first time my father had done this sort of thing, but it hurt as if the scabbed-over wounds had been ripped open again.

Our time there was nice, even if it was a little awkward. Mom and Bobby talked a mile a minute while my father and I sat in uncomfortable silence, contributing to the conversation only when prompted.

When the food was cleared, Bobby began asking my father questions.

"What was it like to run such a huge company like Rickard Published for all those years?"

"It was fine..." he said.

"Did you have a lot of headstrong authors?" he looked at me and winked.

Dad answered matter of factly. "Well, there was always a few."

Finally, after a couple more questions where dad answered like he was sitting on the stand, testifying in court, mom intervened. "You'll have to forgive Liam's father. He lacks some of the basic social graces after spending so many years behind a CEO's desk. Bobby smiled and began talking about his ideas for future books, but the way he answered, I knew he was onto the fact that my father didn't like him.

We left shortly after, and on the way down in the elevator I apologized for my dad. Bobby just laughed.

"Seriously, I'm dating the man's son. Did you think it was going to be all rainbows and strawberries? Clearly, your father thinks it's his job to keep an eye on me. I think it's cute." He leaned over and kissed me before saying, "He really cares about you or he wouldn't be so concerned."

I didn't correct him. It felt good to see the world in the same optimistic way Bobby did. It had been a long time since I'd seen the world as full of goodness, due in large part to the man who'd just slandered him. And only because some fucking asshole, whom Bobby had never met, said so.

We spent the rest of the day making love, eating pizza, and generally enjoying our last day together.

That night, as I held a drowsy Bobby in my arms, I asked when we could see each other again.

He smiled. "Not for a while. I'm going to turn all my devices off when I get to Iowa, drive straight home and finish this book. I don't want to see any other reviews until I do. I'm terrified some will be negative and that'll dampen my excitement."

I smiled. "Tell me about your thoughts."

"Nope, that'll jinx it," he said. "But I'll tell you this much. After meeting your mom's friends, and then Suzie and her family, I've decided there won't be just one superhero, but several working together as a team. Each one having their own special power to save the earth."

I liked the idea of that. It was another twist on the Devereaux style, but definitely not a bad one.

"So, I won't be able to talk to you when you land in Iowa?"

"Nope. I need to escape distractions, and *you* are a major distraction."

"I don't like this plan of yours."

"That's 'cause this is boyfriend Liam talking. Ask CEO Liam what he thinks."

I sighed. "I hate CEO Liam. He has stupid boundaries."

Bobby chuckled and snuggled deeper into me.

"I like both Liams, but for different reasons."

I fell asleep like that, basking in the pure bliss of him. The alarm to get him up and ready for his flight back to Iowa blasted into my consciousness in what felt like just moments after we fell asleep.

"Fuck, this is early, even for me," I said.

"I hate early flights. Who scheduled this for me?"

"That would be Irene. I think I'll fire her when I get to work."

"Fire her for me, too!"

"Deal," I said and fell back asleep while Bobby got up to get his shower.

I drove him to the airport and watched as he disappeared into security. I missed him already.

As I was walking toward my car, I got a text from him.

Miss you!

Yeah, me too! Wanna just come back and stay here?

A little bit, but it's a bad idea.

You've said that before and it didn't stop you.

Well, this time's different, he replied.

Okay, call me when you get home.

No, sorry. I'll be busy. But I'll text you when we land.

I sent him a GIF of a baby sticking his tongue out at someone, and he responded with a laughing emoji.

I felt myself becoming more and more depressed as I drove back to my parents' house. Dragging along the luggage that I'd used while staying with Bobby at the hotel, I went into my room and showered.

Not for the first time since moving out of Atticus' home, I thought it was time to get my own place. The problem was, and always had been, the fact that I didn't want to live alone. It's not like I was ever home anyway, but just knowing my home wasn't empty was why I'd moved back into my parents' apartment to begin with.

As I finished drying off, I decided I should put Irene on the job of getting me my own place. That way, at least when Bobby came into town, he'd have a place to stay other than an impersonal hotel room. And I wouldn't have to be concerned that my father might say something hateful if he came over to my parents' place to visit me.

The day was fine until the newspaper Bobby had worked for released their review of his new book. The critic had lambasted the book as trivial, lacking focus, and a flush of a read.

My heart sank, not only for the company but for Bobby. Of course, I didn't agree with the critic, but he was one of their top reviewers, and I knew a lot of people followed this guy. His reviews were often quoted across the country in various publications.

Remembering my commitment to stay out of things, I called Roy in and showed him the review. Then, I asked him to call Doug and see what they could work out.

"Are you going to call Bobby?" Roy asked.

"No, you're going to call him. That was my agreement with him. Then, you're going to come tell me how he handled it, and after that I'm going to call him."

Roy nodded, then replied, "I don't understand the review. The book was amazing."

I shrugged. "Who knows the mysteries of a critic?"

Later, Roy told me that he'd tried Bobby's number but received no answer. He was concerned that Bobby was upset.

I remembered what Bobby had told me about going off the grid until he got the new story written and filled Roy in on that little fact.

"Make sure to let Doug know as well," I told Roy. "Bobby will probably not want to know about the negative review until after he's done with the first draft."

I couldn't concentrate for the rest of the day, so I took the listings Irene had put together for me and went to find an apartment.

As usual, the pickings in New York were expensive yet bland at best. I finally found a two-bedroom not far from the office. My main criteria was that I could walk to work since I'd want to leave the car parked in the garage at the office.

When I returned, I had Irene set up the lease signing. Then, I arranged for my mom's designer to go in and make sure the place was move-in ready.

I thought about flying to Iowa to let Bobby know about the review personally but immediately dismissed the idea as overkill. My presence would probably make it worse, and I wanted to give him the freedom to get that final book written. If this book tanked now due to this review, I wanted him to have a backup.

As I sat in my office, staring up at the ceiling from my chair, I thought about what this could mean. Was it possible I was about to lose Bobby Devereaux just after I'd gotten him? The thought made my stomach roll and tears prick the backs of my eyes. Sometimes life was just unfair.

Bobby Devereaux

The second I stepped away from Liam and onto the plane, my mind began to construct the story of my third novel. I'd have to go back and rewrite it, adding the new characters. I still wanted the main character to be the powerful political woman who had the power to stand up against the manmade monster, but I wanted her to have support.

Climate change, rising sea levels, melting polar ice caps, and ocean pollution all needed their own superheroes. Maybe I needed to plan future books, giving each of these individuals their own stories. I wanted this one to be about the unsung heroes who stood up to the destruction of the environment in silent ways as much as I wanted it to be about big epic battles with monsters.

The moment I pulled into my driveway, I rushed to unpack. Then I took my computer into my newly updated and renovated office and began writing.

Unlike the first and second novels, this wasn't a rush job. I knew this one needed more finesse. I wanted there to be more nuance to the story. My goal was that someone could read this multiple times and see small details they'd missed the first time.

I knew I was an unusually fast writer. I didn't always have ideas on what to write about, but when a story came to me and it formed itself in my mind, I was able to roll it out fairly quickly.

I'd found that I didn't like distractions. I didn't want to have to socialize with people, take phone calls, or even check texts and emails. I needed to be able to work until the story was done.

The book took two full weeks. Fourteen whole days of intense writing. Of course, my mom showed up after I got home to check on me but when I told her I was in the middle of writing book three she left me alone, only stopping by to bring food over.

When I finally came up for air, I'd rewritten elements of the story multiple times. I'd completely done away with one character I didn't like and then added a minor character who skirted the good and bad issues. It gave more balance to the story, showing how difficult it was to determine right and wrong in the fight against our own environmental indifference.

When I finally finished the last read-through, I was happy. If book two was different from book one, this was an entirely new concept. One that was much more in alignment with who I wanted to be as a writer.

It was just after midnight, so I decided to continue ignoring my phone at least for another night and get some much-needed rest.

When I finally crawled out of bed, I quickly grabbed a shower before going downstairs to get the coffee brewing. I heard my mom's key in the lock just as I was taking my first sip.

She was carrying a tray of food. I rushed over to take it from her and saw biscuits, various breakfast meats, and eggs.

"Mom, are we having a party?" I asked.

"Well, I don't know how long you are going to be writing, so I wanted you to have plenty. You know you forget to eat when you're so focused."

I laughed. "Mom, do people really forget to eat?"

"You do," she said emphatically. "I swear you've always been so hyper-focused. Even when you were little, you'd get into some sort of game or writing in your journal, and if I didn't come get you, you'd have disappeared and died of hunger before you realized you were hungry."

I went over and gave my mom a huge hug and kissed her cheek.

"I'm done," I said and then twirled my mom around the room.

She laughed. "You are amazing!" she said. "You have a whole novel done in just a couple of weeks?"

I laughed. "No, it's far from done. The editors will rip it to shreds and it'll take a while to get it back into shape, but the initial writing is done."

She kissed me and told me to come over for dinner. When I nodded, she gave me another congratulatory hug before going on her way. I fixed myself a breakfast sandwich, put the rest of the food in the refrigerator, and decided to go to the basement to use the workout room I'd installed right before going to New York. I assumed if I spent more time writing, I'd be spending less time on the farm helping my brother, and I didn't want to lose the definition I'd gained while working there.

The weights felt good in my hands. I'd ignored my body for almost three weeks, and I was beginning to feel it. It was almost like my poor muscles were screaming for something to do. After I pushed myself to my limits, each muscle quivering from use, I went back upstairs. Taking a breath, I opened my laptop and began to read the online reviews of my book.

It was confusing at first. Social media was in an uproar. I had to keep scrolling back through hundreds of comments to figure out why everyone was so upset. I finally found out that there was a critic from my previous employer who'd written a negative review about the book. That had set off a firestorm of criticism about the review. I smiled as I scrolled through the comments, as almost all of them were nailing the guy.

I did a Google search for my name and the title and read the more professional commentary. The first few publications had printed his review word for word until the social media response had begun. Then they started to recoil. That was followed by several articles about the negative review and how, according to my fans, the critic had completely missed the mark.

At one point, I leaned back and just laughed. In any other genre, the critic would probably get away with their opinion. In the graphic novel and fantasy world, you could lose your head if the fans didn't agree with you. When I was a kid and saw that someone had criticized Star Trek, my all-time favorite show, I would be the first to take them on for a review I disagreed with. It was important to me.

I called Doug and he was beside himself with concern.

"Dude, do you not read your texts any longer?" he asked.

"Well, hello to you, too, Doug," I said.

"Have you read the review?"

"Yeah, but not until I read the three hundred thousand fan reviews lambasting his."

"Yeah, you've got a strong fan base."

"So, how is this review affecting sales?" I asked.

"It's still only been a couple weeks, but it all looks good from here."

I smiled. "It feels like it's been a lot longer. I finished book three. I think it's my best, but it's different."

Doug sighed. "You're going to be the death of me, Bobby Devereaux. Well, at least we won't have to face those demons until next year. The publishing company probably won't want to release another one until then."

"If they want it. Like I said, it's really different. The hero is different. In fact, this time it's a woman. And there are more characters involved. Think the environmental war equivalent of Marvel's *The Avengers.*

"Send it over. I'll give it a read. Have you already sent it to Roy?" he asked.

"Not this time. You were my first phone call after coming out of the writing fog."

"Well, that's a nice change," he said sarcastically.

As I was talking, I pressed send on the email I'd already begun writing when he picked up my call.

"You should be getting it any moment," I replied. "Have you heard from Liam?"

As soon as I asked, I regretted it.

Doug chuckled. "You know I've heard from Liam, but he's trying to stay out of it because of some agreement you two made. So, when he calls, it's all, *'How are you doing, Doug? What's a good place for breakfast close to your office?'*. It's cute."

I smiled, getting sweet butterflies in my stomach as I thought about the guy trying to honor our agreement but desperately wanting to know more about what's going on.

"Did you tell him you hadn't spoken to me, at least?"

"Nope. Figured I'd let Roy keep him informed."

"Speaking of you and Roy, how's that going?"

Doug was silent for a moment. "What do you know?"

"Oh, Doug, everyone knows. You and Roy have been sniffing around each other for years. I noticed while I was there that you two seemed closer. I meant to bring it up, but things moved too fast."

Doug sighed. "Well, he moved in with me."

I yelled into the phone like a schoolgirl whose best friend had just told her that a boy had asked her to go steady. "You dog! And you two didn't tell me? How long?"

"He moved in shortly after you left. Are you mad?"

"No, of course not. I'm glad it finally worked out for you two. Has he told Liam yet?"

"Yeah, last week while you were MIA."

"What was Liam's reaction?"

"Mixed feelings. Mostly I think he was happy for Roy. You know he promoted him again? He's now running the entire graphic novel section of the company. Roy told me with the success you've had, they now want to recruit more writers in the genre."

"Cool. I'll call Liam after work and get the lowdown."

Doug promised to read my book and get back to me with his initial reactions, which would be strange. I hadn't considered that Doug might have ideas he wanted me to iron out before sending the story to Roy. Doug was smart, had his ear to the rails, and knew better than most what the fans would think about the story. I felt a bit of a thrill knowing I'd have one more layer of support, with him looking over things, before sending it on to Roy.

I sent a text to Liam then, telling him I was done hibernating and desperate to hear his voice.

I got a text back instantly.

Want me to fly to Iowa?

Yeah, but it would be sort of crazy. Don't you have a lot going on with that new Devereaux book I heard something about? I teased.

Sorry, forgot. I'm being boyfriend Liam. I laughed.

Sorry for the bad review.

Part of the game. Sounds like it isn't hurting sales, though.

That's something you'll have to talk to CEO Liam about.

You are funny. Can you call me?

Nope. I'm in a boring meeting from hell. I'll call when I can.

Okay.

I almost texted *love you* but stopped myself. It was so strange. I blew it off as me just being used to saying it to my mom or siblings, even to my friends when we texted. I've never been afraid of sharing emotions with those I cared about. But you didn't tell your boyfriend you loved him, even in a text, until you were sure it was...more.

I ran into town and bought groceries since, other than the food my mom had graciously brought me, my refrigerator looked like a desert. As I was pulling back into my driveway, I got the call from Liam.

"Hey, sexy. How's it going?"

"It's crazy. How's your life?"

"Weird. It's always hard to get back into the swing of things after being out of it for a week or two. I hear you're creating a new division in Rickards."

"Yeah, been in the works for a while. The board likes how well your books are doing. They want to try promoting this new direction. Just so you know, I blame you for the endless boring meetings I'm having to sit through as they drone on and on about it."

I *hmphed*, then said, "You love it and you know it."

"Yeah, a little bit. I love that it's your writing that's spinning the development."

"So, Roy's going to head it?" I asked.

"You've been gossiping with Doug, haven't you?"

"Yeah, and since they're now boyfriends, that makes it that much more interesting."

"More than boyfriends. Did Doug tell you they're living together?"

"He did. Do you realize that we're a couple of ninnies gossiping about them?"

He laughed. "Just catching up, not gossiping."

"Uh-huh..."

"I miss you," he said, out of the blue.

"Yeah, I miss you, too. Well, I do now. You'd be a horrible distraction if I were still trying to write."

"So, you're saying if I were to come visit, you wouldn't be able to write while I'm there?"

"That's exactly what I'm saying. But I'd be happy to take a break while you're here."

He was silent for a moment.

"Have you ever thought of moving back to New York?"

"No, Liam. It wasn't a good experience last time I lived there. You've heard about all the crap I went through with Randy."

"Yeah, I know. But I've got my own apartment and wondered if you'd consider coming to stay here with me? At least occasionally."

I looked around my newly renovated home and sighed.

"Iowa winters are pretty bad, so maybe I could spend time in New York to escape the winters here. But only if you commit to coming here some as well."

"That's a no-brainer. Yes and double yes. But I'm not working with the nasty pigs. I deal with enough shit here. I don't want to deal with it there."

I laughed. "Nobody would expect you to help on the farm. What would you do while you were here, though?"

"I'd work just like I do here. I don't have to attend all these meetings. They just pile them on me 'cause I'm conveniently available. Most of what I do is endless paperwork, and Irene can send all that to me."

"I'm sure Irene would love for you to be gone for a while, anyway."

"Nah, she'd miss me. Maybe we could have her come out, too. I bet she'd help you on your family's pig farm."

"No doubt." I heard something in the background and knew she was fussing about us talking about her behind her back.

Liam responded with something about boundaries, but I could hear the humor in his voice.

When he came back on the phone, he asked, "Do you think you could come back in a week or so? I have a designer working on my apartment, but since you might be staying with me, maybe you could offer some opinions about décor."

"Liam, it's your apartment. You should decide how it looks."

"Yeah, but would you look over the designs, at least?"

I shrugged, even though he couldn't see me.

"You can have the designer send stuff to me and I'll look at it, but it's weird."

"It's not weird that I'm asking my boyfriend what he thinks of my design choices."

"If you say so. Anyway, I should let you get back to your work. I'm going to take a nap, then run over to my parents' place."

"It must be nice. I haven't had a nap since...well, since you were here."

"I'm still catching up on sleep from the last two weeks. But, yeah, it's nice. And now I'm going to think about you snuggling with me while I'm napping."

Liam sighed. "I miss you."

"I miss you too. Now go work!"

We hung up and I went upstairs to crash in bed. I needed to strip the sheets and do laundry, but I was tired and decided I'd do that the next day.

What would it be like to spend time in New York again? Before last week, I'd have flat-out refused, but spending time with Liam's mother, Tiffany and her friends had changed my outlook on that segment of society. They were fun, funny, engaging, and I genuinely enjoyed them.

Spending time with Suzie Freemont and her family had been amazing. I wondered if we'd hang out more often if I decided to come back to town. I liked that thought. I loved Eddie, and of course, now that he and Sabastian were a thing, I could see some double dates in our future. But I needed more than just fashion industry queens to keep me functioning in New York for the long term.

It would be fun to introduce them to Clay and Denim, though...if they weren't already acquainted. It seemed like Eddie knew everyone in New York. At least, anyone who wore designer clothing.

Hands down, though, the best part about being back in the city would be Liam, his long muscular arms wrapped around me, his smooth, hard body spooned against me. I fell asleep with thoughts of the man holding me and had really pleasant dreams.

Liam Rickard

D ivorce, Mom? Really?"

She looked at me with sad eyes. "I'm afraid that's not the most difficult news, honey. Sit down for a moment."

I'd been pacing behind her big leather sofa since she'd told me that she and Dad had decided to split up and that he'd officially moved out of the apartment.

I hesitantly did as she asked.

"You know we both love you, but things are complicated, especially for those of us who grew up in the eighties. The world was less accepting of different lifestyles."

I was beginning to get a clue where this was headed, so I asked, "Mom, are you a lesbian?"

I'd surprised her, and she let out a laugh.

"No, I love men. But your father is bisexual." She let that sink in for a moment.

"Mom, that's crazy! He has *Playboy* magazines all over his bedroom."

"Well, bisexual means he likes both men and women. I've always known. He dated a man before he dated me, even though it was taboo back then. Then we fell in love and I couldn't imagine not being his wife. He was faithful to me until we stopped being intimate. That's been a while. He just stopped being..."

She looked at me, sadness quickly draining from her expression.

"Well, that's more information than you need. But what you do need to know is he didn't date anyone else while we were intimate, and he was always honest when he met someone. Your dad might be a lot of things, but he never cheated on me, and he never lied to me. I think you need to know that before I go on."

I looked at her suspiciously. "Mom, why didn't you or he ever tell me? Hell, I came out to you when I was sixteen."

She shook her head. "Well, at the time, we were still a couple. When he started seeing men again, it was more of an experiment. We were separated, but neither of us wanted to tell others until it was official."

"It seems so odd, Mom. I'm having a hard time processing it." I started to stand, and she put her hand on my leg to stop me.

"Your father is with Atticus," she said.

My stomach flipped and I felt sick.

"Mom, please tell me that's not true."

She looked a little green herself but kept her hand on my knee. "I'm sorry, honey."

I went to the kitchen, got myself a glass of water, and came back to the couch. I needed to know the whole story. As sordid as it was, I needed to know.

"Atticus was fucking my dad and me at the same time?" I asked.

She shook her head. "No, your father had been resisting his advances. I'm not sure if they were intimate before or not, but from what your father has told me, I don't think they had been. But when your father refused him, he pursued you instead."

Everything began to make sense, then. Atticus's interest in me, my father's anger about me dating him.

"I feel like I'm going to be sick. Mom, why didn't you tell me?"

"I didn't know about Atticus until much later. When I confronted your father about why he was acting so strange, he told me he wasn't involved with him. I didn't want to crush you, and you needed an advocate at the time because you were so hurt by how your dad had rejected you. I didn't know what to do."

I sighed. "So, what's changed now? Why are you leaving him after all this time?"

Her face was pale. All she could say was, "Atticus." She took a deep breath and continued. "When he told me, I asked him to leave. They are living together."

I barely made it to the toilet before my stomach emptied. I couldn't get past the thought of that horrible man sleeping with my father. It was more than I could take. More than my stomach could take.

I rinsed my mouth out and went into my old bedroom to lie down. I silently thanked the Universe that I was moving out. I couldn't stay here now I'd learned all that.

I don't know how long I was lying there before I heard Mom come in and sit on the bed next to me. She rubbed my hair like she'd done when I was little, and the touch triggered the tears.

"He knows what that man did to me, yet he's still doing this?"

She didn't respond but kept rubbing my hair.

I turned over and looked at her. "Mom, why didn't he tell me?"

She shrugged, and said, "*C'est un lâche.*"

"Yeah, he is a coward. A big, fat, nasty coward."

Mom rarely fell back into French. She played the perfect American housewife and that role had done well for my parents when they were growing the publishing company to its current size. She only switched to French when she was emotional. If she yelled at you in French, it was time to hide because you'd pushed her too far.

Her use of it now was enough to show me how much this hurt her as well.

"What are you going to do?" I said, lying back down.

"I'm going to go back to the vineyard for a while. Since you are moving out, I want to sell the apartment. I don't want him living here with Atticus."

The thought turned my stomach again. "I agree. Will he sign off on the sale?"

She nodded. "Yeah, we've already discussed it. When we separated years back, we drew up a plan for divorce. It's already worked out."

"I'd like to come to the vineyard after you've had some time to heal. I've been wanting to visit Uncle Josué and Aunt Esmee."

"Maybe you can bring Bobby when you come. I'd like to see him again, but not for a while, okay? I need some time to figure out what I'm doing with my life."

I nodded and she leaned over, kissing me on the temple before she left the room.

I fell asleep, the impact of everything I'd just learned coursing through me. When I woke up, the apartment was empty. I wished Bobby were with me. I desperately wanted him here.

On a whim, I texted him and asked if it would be okay for me to visit.

Although it was late, he texted back moments later. Yes, YES! Can you come now?

Even though I was sick after the news about my dad, he was still able to make me smile.

I boarded the earliest flight out the next morning and was met at Des Moines airport by the brightest ray of sunshine in my life. The moment he was in my arms, I knew I was going to be okay.

I managed to get through baggage claim and into his truck. He looked at me with concern, and when I just shook my head after he asked what was wrong, I felt the tears start up again. I was mortified, but it didn't make any difference. The tears had a mind of their own. He scooted across the seat and pulled me into a hug.

"Shh, it's okay, it's going to be okay," he said as I emptied my emotions onto him.

When I finally got myself under control enough that I could move away from him, he asked if I wanted to go somewhere to talk or drive back to his home.

"I don't think public is a good idea at the moment," I said, and he nodded.

As we drove the two hours to his house, I told him about everything that had happened. He looked at me with confusion, then empathy.

"Geez, that's awful. I'm so sorry."

"Thank you," I replied. "I probably shouldn't have come, but I needed to get away and my mom is going to France to be with her family. I didn't know where else to go."

"I'm glad you came here," he said. "I like the idea of being able to take care of you. Besides, now that I'm done with the manuscript, I'm bored out of my mind."

I looked at him, shocked. "You're done with the editing?" I asked.

He smiled and nodded. "Well, on this end at least. Doug is reading over it before he submits it to you officially, so you have to register all this on the boyfriend side of our relationship. He'll be upset if he finds out I told you."

"You think he hasn't already told Roy?"

He shrugged. "I don't know. It's all confusing. I've not actually used him this way before. I've always just sent my work straight to Roy when I was done. But I do like that Doug can look it over before Roy gets it. It's like another layer of review."

"Yeah, it's how most people do it."

"Most people aren't having awesome sex with the CEO of their publishing company."

"No, probably not," I agreed.

We rode quietly the rest of the way back.

"Mom said she'd have us over for dinner tonight, but I think we'll hold off for now. Unless you think you're ready to be around people."

I shook my head. "No. Sorry. I don't think I could do socializing right now. Mostly I need to hibernate and snuggle with you."

"I've missed that," he said, smiling at me.

"Yeah, me, too. I think I need that more than anything right now."

I was amazed when we drove up to the house. It had been transformed. The outside had been painted, and flowerbeds were being prepped for gardens around the home and along the sidewalk up to the house. There was a swing on the front porch as well as a couple rocking chairs facing it.

When I walked inside, the living space was also completely different. There was a new kitchen, the hardwood floors had been refinished and ran throughout the open concept layout.

"It's beautiful," I said, turning in circles to see everything.

"I made my brother help me, but I also hired a lot of it out. You like it?" Bobby asked.

"I love it. I have to admit, I didn't see this in my mind's eye when I thought about coming to visit. I anticipated the cold, run-down farmhouse."

"And you still came here. That says a lot about your current mental state."

"I prefer this to the way it was," I admitted, and he smiled.

He gave me a tour, including his new workout space in the basement. He'd combined two rooms upstairs to create a nice master and en suite. The room I'd stayed in last time had been converted into an office with luxurious furniture and a writing desk.

I followed him to another bedroom, almost the exact same size as the other one. It was completely empty.

"This is your office if you want it."

I looked at him, perplexed. "What do you mean *my* office?"

"Well, you said you could work while you're here, so I set this space up for you. We just need to furnish it when you're ready to work."

I came over and pulled him into a hug. Another tear slipped from me, but I quickly wiped it away. That one was a happy tear, but after all the sad ones, I didn't want Bobby to get confused and think I wasn't beyond thankful he'd done this for me.

I spent an entire week with Bobby, Irene pushing all my meetings to the following week.

We spent most days in our opposite corners working in the gentle sunlight that poured through both our office windows. Then he'd bring me lunch, or we'd meet down in the kitchen.

Being with him felt magical. His sweet attention and caring nature made me feel like a new human being. The wounds my father inflicted, although far from healed, began to feel manageable.

We spent time with his family and I found I liked them. They were smart and witty. They teased us relentlessly, but they were also a solid wall of strength behind him. Seeing their unwavering support made my heart hurt more at first, knowing my father had pretty much ripped that element out of our family when he decided to have an affair with my ex.

By the time I got on the plane to fly back east, I felt almost human again. Mom had sent all my stuff to my new apartment before she'd flown to France. She'd put her apartment on the market, and the last text she'd sent me was to let me know that they had an interested buyer. Real estate in New York didn't last, so I had no doubt it'd be gone quickly enough.

I went to the office after getting home, where I got my new keys from Irene. She pulled me into an uncharacteristic hug.

"I'm sorry you're going through this," she said, which made the emotions swell inside me before I could tamp them back down.

"Thanks, Irene. I appreciate that."

My new apartment made me feel better. Bobby had made a few suggestions about layout and design, which I'd shared with the designer. Knowing he'd been involved made me feel like he was here with me in some way. The designer had integrated some stuff from my old bedroom, and what she hadn't used, she'd stored in my closet. There was a huge storage closet in the apartment that hadn't been there when I was looking at the place, and I put a reminder in my phone to send the designer a thank you card and flowers because the extra storage was amazing. I also noticed there was an entire section of the closet available for my significant other to store his things. I couldn't wait until Bobby filled it with his stuff.

If Bobby had lived in New York, I doubted I would've been so quick to share my living space. Of course, I say that but I also have to acknowledge I'd moved back home because I didn't want to live alone. Bobby living more than a thousand miles away did make me less concerned about sharing the space. However, having space especially for him felt right.

Thinking of the office space we'd designed for me at his house while I was visiting, I took several pictures of the new place, including his empty closet space, and texted them to him.

When are you coming to fill that empty closet space up? I asked.

He sent back a smiley emoji.

Soon.

Soon, ended up being two weeks later, when he came to town and spent a week with me.

The second I saw him at the airport, I pulled him into my arms and kissed him passionately not caring who saw us. "God, I missed you," I admitted and noted how cute Bobby was when he blushed in my embrace.

He nuzzled into me and laid his head on my shoulder. "Yeah, I missed you too."

When I wasn't at work, I showed him some of my favorite parts of New York.

There were parts of northern Central Park where the tourists didn't seem to go, and I had a few favorite restaurants up there that I was able to show him as well. The park was always wonderful, no matter what part you were in but when you could wander around without the large crowds, it filled the soul.

I loved that New York, for the most part, was safe for a gay couple to show affection. We wandered through shops that surrounded the park. He'd look for different birds and geek out about those that migrated through the area this time of year.

We made another stop in Little Italy and Chinatown, but this time we ate Asian food at a restaurant I'd enjoyed long ago while I was still in college. Bobby's demeanor was different than the first time we'd come to this area of town. While we were at odds before, we seemed to be perfectly matched now. That feeling left me overwhelmed and deeply satisfied at the same time.

Too soon, the week was over. I swiped at an errant tear when he pulled away from me to go into the airport alone. "It's like tearing my heart out when you leave," I said and Bobbly sadly nodded.

That was the way our summer unfolded. Bobby flew to his agreed-upon book tours and Comic-Cons and I'd try to join him when I could get away. Each time we parted it felt like my heart was being cleaved in to.

We managed to steal a week here and there throughout the summer, but by late fall, I was desperate to spend more time with Bobby. I texted him shortly after he walked into the secure part of the airport, asking him if he'd consider coming to stay longer than just a week.

"No, I need to be home to help Louis once mom and dad leave for Florida. Besides, we're spending Christmas together. It'll be here before you know it. Think about it, you'll get to meet my entire family and in the Florida sun nonetheless."

As I got back into my car to leave before security got onto me for staying in the drop-off zone, I wondered how the hell this man had come to mean so much to me in such a short time.

Mom had flown back into town and was packing up her apartment so the sale could be finalized. We both shed a few tears. I longed for Bobby to be here so I'd have someone to curl into when the day ended.

Luckily, as we worked through the apartment, I still hadn't seen my father since finding out he and Atticus were together. After all the stuff was put in storage and the sale of the apartment was completed, Mom agreed to stay with me for a few days before flying back to France.

Unfortunately, the day after the apartment sold the proverbial shit hit the fan. I started getting texts from people I hadn't heard from in years about a tell-all by local gossip columnist Jessie Hubbard. I finally went to a link one of my dad's acquaintances sent me.

The social media post basically described a mostly fabricated sordid tale of how my father had moved into the home of my ex, Atticus Sterling.

"In a wave of sexual trysts and scandalous partner sharing, these men jumped from one bed to another and all the while Atticus and Randy were committed to other people."

The post also hinted that my dad and I had some sort of incestuous relationship as well. Although, if you read it closely it didn't out-and-out say that, making it difficult for anybody to sue him for libel.

What did help, at least in the grand scheme of things, was that Jessie disclosed that Atticus was friends with the man who had published the negative review of Bobby's book. Apparently, Randy had talked Atticus into convincing his friend to give Bobby a bad review because of the perceived slight Bobby had given him and Jessie at the Save the Ocean gala.

I ignored the rest of the article and forwarded it to the company's attorney, asking what, if anything, could be done. I put special emphasis on the defamatory review.

I found Mom in the guest room. "I assume you've seen all this."

She laughed. "Honey, it's awful, but it serves your father right for getting involved with such trash."

I smiled at the sound of her French accent that had come out in full bloom at the scandal.

"May I recommend you go spend some time away and let all this pass?" she asked. "I'm going to take an earlier flight back to France and dance naked among the vines thinking about how karma is a bitch and how much I love her."

"Mother," I said squeamishly.

"Don't be prudish, son," she replied, laughing, then started speaking in French about the scandal and how I needed to spend time in my mother country.

I laughed. "Okay, Mom. I'll come to France and we can celebrate the scandal with wine!"

"Good," she said. "I'm done with this stuffy life."

I knew this was all part of her healing process, and I was happy she was taking the scandal with such grace.

I called Bobby next and told him the latest news regarding the scandal. He laughed about the review.

"That reviewer won't be able to show his face again. The Comic-Con fans are going to fillet him."

"Agreed. I'm also having our attorney look into what can be done legally since the review was intentionally libelous and could impact sales."

Bobby just shrugged that off, saying I could do whatever I wanted to do. "In the end, I get the guy, so who cares?"

"So, you want to take a trip to France?" I asked. "I've got to get away from here to avoid making the scandal worse, and I'd prefer not to go where reporters will figure out where we're at. Oh, and that reminds me, don't talk to reporters."

"You think they'll find me in middle-of-nowhere Iowa?"

"Oh, I have no doubt they'll find you there. This is a big deal, Bobby and not just legally. Everyone in New York will be talking about it."

"Yes then. I'll come to France with you. But we have to be back for Christmas. I promised my folks I was bringing you with me to Florida."

"That's weeks away. I'll have Irene set up the flight and meet you here in New York before we fly to Paris."

"Oh. That reminds me. If we are going to be in Paris, I want to see Aiden Fisher's exhibit in the

Louvre. Do you think we can spend a weekend there first?"

"Yes, that's perfect. I'll have Irene arrange it."

When I hung up, I was in a great mood. I wasn't sure why. Jessie had insinuated we were all having incestuous affairs, but I doubted anyone was going to believe him in the long run. Once my attorneys filed the first lawsuit, the reporters would switch from speculation to ferreting out the facts. No one wanted a powerful New York family having their attorneys working them over. Hell hath no fury like a scandalized rich person.

Bobby Devereaux

I promised we'd be back from France in time for Christmas three times before my mom let me go. She looked like she was about to cry.

"Mom, seriously, I'll be back. I'll leave early to make sure I can get back in time for the holiday and avoid the crowds. And I've already booked a cabin at your campground in Florida. So, we'll be together, I promise!"

"If you promise, honey. I just want to have you home." Mom was a master at playing the mom card. Even if I hadn't been planning to come home, I'm sure I would've after the expression she gave me.

I flew to New York and Liam met me at the airport.

"Hi," he said when after we embraced.

"Hi back," I said, smiling at how wonderful it was to be back in his arms. There was a five-hour layover, but we spent it together talking about the new book and the scandal.

"So," I began, then looked over at Liam. "How're you doing with all the stuff about your dad and your ex and well... my ex?" I asked and Liam smiled sadly.

"I'm guessing it'll be a heck of a lot harder on my dad than anyone else," he replied, the sadness still clear in his voice.

I hugged him again knowing this was hard for him. But, ultimately, he seemed to be taking it in good humor.

When we landed in Paris, Liam had dinner set up for us and after we'd eaten, we turned in for the night. Both of us dealing with a little jet lag.

The next day was...well, it was Paris. I'd never been before, so Liam took me to all the sites. We spent a week touring the city since neither of us had to work. Liam had taken a leave of absence for the next three weeks, so he was not scheduled to return until after the holidays. That didn't stop Irene from texted him constantly.

"Um, aren't you supposed to be on leave?" I asked as we stood gazing across the River Seine at the reconstruction of Notre Dame.

Liam laughed then kissed me. "I'm never on leave, but I'll tell Irene to hold off a bit if you want."

"I want. Look, Liam. We're standing in one of the most iconic parts of the world and you can't stop texting."

He put his arm around me and pulled me into his side.

"It's such a shame that she's gone," Liam said, changing the subject to address the cathedral.

"Did you get to see it before it burned?"

"Yeah, several times and we toured it too when mom would bring me here over the holidays."

I snuggled closer and sighed, mourning the fact that I'd never had the chance to see the historic beauty in her original ancient splendor.

We toured art museums and I learned how much Liam loved art. The Louvre was spectacular. Not just because of the priceless art, but because the architecture of the pyramid was art itself.

Liam laughed at me as I sighed when I saw the Mona Lisa in person. Although, as everyone says, it's smaller than you'd think. We stood in line for an hour to get a glimpse of her, but it was worth every moment.

'Hey, do you want to see Aiden Fisher's collection, now?" he asked.

"Of course!" I exclaimed.

The exhibit was tucked away in a gallery for living artists, surrounded by interesting paintings and modern sculpture. But Aiden's collection stood above and beyond the rest. There was a line nowhere near as long as Mona Lisa's, but a line nonetheless, and we waited to view the notorious piece that belonged to Aiden's husband, Devin. It was only displayed once a year for a short time as a part of the agreement between the gallery and Devin. Of course, it was so romantic that tourists tended to flock to the Louvre to see it when it showed up each year.

The piece was lovely, small like the Mona Lisa, but impressive nonetheless. After seeing the collection, I felt a little more star-struck with Aiden Fisher than I had when we'd met in the little diner in New York.

We wandered around the sites of Paris. Luckily after I took the phone away from Liam and texted Irene telling her I was confiscating his phone so he could enjoy the city with me, she stopped texting. Okay, she stopped texting as much.

I let Liam spoil me. We ate at swanky French restaurants that had terraces and sidewalk tables. People sat around us, some couples, some individuals, everyone engrossed in their own little worlds.

"You're making me a wine snob," I said the following afternoon as we sat on the riverbank and drank a bottle of expensive French wine.

"Good," he stated smugly, picking up a piece of the cheese and plopping it into my mouth before kissing me.

"Why is it everything about Paris is delicious, wine, bread, pastries...sex?"

Liam kissed me again and let me lean against him as we watched the people walk past us.

Finally, I sat up and said, "The air in Paris must be laced with something."

"Like what?" Liam asked chuckling.

"Like pheromones or something. I swear I've never wanted to kiss anyone as much as I want to kiss you here."

"We should find out what it is, so we can install it in my apartment when you come to visit." He teased me.

"You'd never get any work done," I said, completely serious.

Each night, we'd end up twined around each other making passionate love. Almost as if we were delirious with desire.

By the time we headed south to his aunt and uncle's vineyard, I felt like a different man.

Usually, being in a large city made people more anxious and frazzled. Paris seemed to have the opposite effect. As we rode the train out of the city, I left feeling Parisian.

The train ride to the vineyard between Bordeaux and Bergerac took just under two hours, but unlike traveling in the states, traveling by train was almost as wonderful as arriving.

I couldn't say I wasn't shocked by Liam's aunt and uncle. Liam's mom was the definition of refinement, perfect from her incredible shoes to her coiffed hair.

Her brother and his wife were anything but. They both wore work clothes and spoke in graveled voices that indicated years of smoking.

"Your home is spectacular," I said as I entered the old villa. The couple smiled when Liam translated for me.

My compliment was the understatement of the century as I wandered through a property that looked more like it should be on television in one of those romantic movies from the middle of the last century.

I was concerned that I wouldn't fit in with this European family, but my fears were quickly waylaid as we bonded over the similarities that people who worked the land tend to share.

Although I had taken French in college and had friends from Tahiti, I'd never learned the language well enough to speak it fluently.

As a result, communicating when Liam or his mother wasn't around was a bit challenging. Despite that, when Liam's uncle Josué found out that I lived and worked on a hog farm, he took me to tour his friend's farm just down the road from his estate.

I had to work hard to understand, but after he repeated himself once more I finally got that Josué was saying, "France is the third largest producer of swine in the EU."

Then his friend turned into a salesman.

"If you have experience," he said in English with a thick accent, "and open a hog farm here, they will give you capital to start."

I laughed.

"Thank you, but I'm a writer, not a farmer," I said.

Liam wandered over to where we were standing then and interpreted when he looked confused. The older man's face fell and when we left Liam's uncle explained. "There is fear from the older generation that there won't be enough farmers in the future to keep up with the demand."

I chuckled to myself when I thought of my brother and his wife crossing the ocean from Iowa to settle on a farm in the middle of France.

It only took a moment before I'd fallen for the vineyard and its surrounding agricultural region as much as I had for Paris.

As Liam and I laid in the small bedroom tucked in the far corner of the house, I whispered, "I could easily spend months here."

"What would you do?" he asked.

"Humm, write, tour vineyards, dairy operations, and other farms."

"Well, since mom is living here now, we might have to do that."

All too soon, it was time to leave. I felt bad that I'd barely spent any time with Tiffany. She was a hive of activity, though. She'd spent a good deal of time visiting friends she'd gone to school with and had gone on several outings to other vineyards where she sampled the wine. When she got back, she always gave her opinions to her brother, comparing the quality between his wine and theirs.

I knew she was still struggling with her breakup and being busy was good for her, but I missed spending time with her and talking about all the environmental stuff we were both committed to fixing.

Once we left Tiffany in France, we didn't fly to Florida right away. Instead, we flew back to New York and went to Liam's apartment so he could replenish his wardrobe and prepare for Florida's warmer climate.

I was so happy we'd come home early. We basically slept for the first full day, getting up only to have a little food or watch TV.

After arriving in Florida and settling in, we went to my parents' RV for dinner. Mom made plans for the Christmas meal, assigning us each something to bring. When she found out poor Liam was useless in the kitchen, she said he'd have potato and egg peeling duty.

"What's that?" he asked me quietly when she left the room.

"It's grunt labor. Everyone hates the job."

"Oh great, I see where you get your masochistic ways."

When I looked at him questioningly, he said, "*Pig poop puddle*," and I got it. My brother Louis overheard our conversation, and from that point on the incident became known as the PPP, the pig poop puddle incident. From then on, Louis stopped tiptoeing around the nasty PPP and harassed Liam about it freely

It was great being with family, and Liam fit in like he'd been a part of us from day one.

For Christmas dinner, since I hadn't been able to join them for Thanksgiving, Mom and Dad rented the reception hall at the campground, which had a big commercial kitchen, so we didn't all have to try to fit into their RV.

Mom's family flew down to join us as well, and although my grandma, uncle, and aunt were strict Catholics, they didn't seem to have a problem with Liam or me.

"So, how does it feel to have the writer of a movie star book on your arm?" my aunt asked Liam as we sat down for dinner that night.

Liam looked over at me, affection dripping from him and shrugged. "Just like you would think it feels."

Uncle Louis clapped me on the shoulder when dinner was over and said, "Your grandma was so proud of you that she put the poster of the movie above the mantle." He looked at mom, then his sister and said, "We also have the newspaper clipping of you at the première in a nice frame as well."

She'd always had a huge gold framed mirror in that space while I was growing up, and I couldn't quite imagine what a movie poster would look like there. By the look on my aunt's face, who now lived with grandma, it didn't look all that great.

As we sat around the huge table, I thought this was as good as it could get. A happy, well-rounded family, and a man I was pretty sure I'd fallen in love with

.

Liam Rickard

As amazing as the last few weeks had been, my return home was equally horrible. The rumors hadn't gone away, they'd only spread. Luckily, the accusation of incest had basically disappeared, but the scandal of my father dating my ex, along with me dating the ex of the same guy who was having an affair with my ex, who was with my father...well, it was a lot of ugly that reconstituted itself over and over.

Irene texted me and told me my presence was being requested at the board meeting the next day. That couldn't be good. Since I'd begun improving our brand, the board had been mostly hands-off. Between my dad, my mom, and my stocks in the company, we still had a majority share but that didn't mean we couldn't be manipulated.

I sat at the head of the long boardroom table while the old farts my father had put on the board long ago told me they'd decided I should step down. My father abstained, declining to cast his vote either way, so, even with my mom's votes, I'd been canned.

The news was devastating. I felt sick. I'd let the company become all-consuming in my life, even though I had long ago grown bored with the ins and outs. The only thing that really inspired me was working with Bobby and our plans to expand the brand to include more graphic novels. Which incidentally, my new boyfriend was pretty excited about too.

Unfortunately, my job wasn't the only thing the rumor was affecting. The rumors continued to get worse and worse, and at one point they began affecting Bobby's sales. I paced for two days straight, never able to get my mind off the fact that my dad's poor decisions were going to end up tanking Bobby's book.

***

I couldn't eat. If I'm honest, I wasn't even really functioning like a human being. My dad's ridiculous choices were going to ruin us all. But the thing I perseverated on, unable to get it out of my head, was how this was affecting Bobby.

I knew what I had to do. The only way I could save the man I loved more than I loved anything else at this point in my life was to let him go. I had to break up with him.

My entire system rebelled at the choice, but I had to save him. I had to keep him from being pulled down into this mess. After agonizing over the thought, the week after New Years', I called.

"Hello handsome," Bobby's chipper voice answered on the second ring.

"Hi, Bobby, we need to talk."

"Yes, hey, before I forget, mom wanted me to ask if you can come spend a week with us in July. We just heard that the Iowa bike ride called RAGBRI is coming through our town. Dad wants to sell pulled pork bar-be-que."

Just a few days ago, planning to spend a week with him and his family would've melted my heart but the knowledge of what could be lost if I didn't sever ties prompted me forward.

"No, Bobby. No, I can't! We can't keep this up."

I was trying to talk fast now, hoping that he wouldn't say anything else that might make this harder than it already was.

Bobby laughed, "You think you're funny. You can't get rid of me that easy boss man."

The tears were streaming down my face now. I couldn't help if he didn't understand. I had to cut this and I had to do it now.

"I'm sorry, Bobby, it's over."

I hung up, unable to bear his reaction when he understood I wasn't joking. I know I'm a coward, but no one has ever meant as much to me as Bobby did.

Letting him go was like having my heart filleted while it was still beating in my chest.

That was the worst time of my life. Even worse than the entire mess with Atticus. My mom was in France, my dad was still holed up, God only knew where, and I was alone, no friends, no boyfriend, and unemployed.

Bobby had tried to call and text repeatedly. I knew, or at least I was almost sure, that if he was going to release this next book and have the success he deserved, he couldn't be associated with me and my pariah family.

Irene came over, even dragging poor Doug and Roy with her a couple times. I mostly ignored them. It was two weeks after breaking up with the love of my life that Irene showed up alone. She brought groceries and a bottle of wine.

"Liam, you have to get out of this apartment. It's not good for you. Why don't you call Bobby and ask him to come here, or better yet, you can go there."

I shook my head and she sighed before picking up her phone. "In that case I'll call him myself."

I grabbed the phone from her. "No, we broke up."

"What's that you say?" Irene's accent rarely showed up. Usually only when she was excited or trying to rib me, but it also showed up when she was upset.

"We broke up. I had to Irene. His book sales were tanking, and it was because of me."

"Oh, that's nonsense, Liam. Call him right now and tell him you made a mistake."

"I won't ruin his life, Irene. I won't be why he loses his career."

We both sat silently. The tears slipping down my face and her staring at me like I'd lost my mind.

Finally, she handed me a couple tissues. "I think this is a huge mistake. You should reconsider."

I shook my head. In the end, Irene left but not before spending the best part of an hour trying to convince me to see the error of my ways. Ultimately I just said, "I love him too much to see him destroyed by all this...stuff!

I realized after she left that the only friends I had were the ones from Rickard Publishing. That was pathetic...*I* was pathetic.

Night after night, I paced my living room floor. Irene's argument repeating itself over and over in my head.

I need to pull away from him, right? I'd had the same argument over and over again. I'd almost convince myself to go back and beg him to forgive me, then I'd think about the fact that me and the baggage of my family could destroy his career, and I'd back out.

I watched as various media sites announced our breakup. Roy had assured me *that* in itself had bumped Bobby's sales up.

That was the confirmation I needed. Bobby deserved more than me. Better than me. And I needed to step away and let him be.

After languishing in my apartment, I finally decided I was done with New York. It was time for a change. I flew back to France to be close to my mom and the only family I trusted.

Bobby Devereaux

I liked to think I'm an independent person, but when Liam broke up with me out of the blue, I was devastated. Unlike when I'd left Randy, I was more depressed than I'd ever been before. I'd unfortunately fallen completely and utterly in love with Liam Rickard.

I closed off his office in my house and locked the old 1920s door. It felt like just having the room open gave him the power to hurt me again.

I lost count of how many days I lay in bed before my family intervened. Mom came in first. "Honey, it's not good for you to lay around. Why don't you come to the house for supper tonight?"

I sat up when she came in, but I just shrugged. "I'm sorry, mom. I don't think I can right now."

Dad and Louis must've been listening at the door because they came in and dad said, "Nope, you aren't going to lay here and waste away." and then looked over at Louis. "Do we need to have your brother pick you up and drag you down the stairs?"

I slumped down to the kitchen my whole body feeling like it'd been broken piece by piece.

I cried like I hadn't done since I was little. My parents took turns holding me. After that, either Louis, Mom, Dad or Clair would stay with me. My pride, under normal circumstances, would've forced them to leave me alone. But the truth was, I'd never hurt like this before. I needed them.

I don't know when, but maybe sometime after a couple of weeks, I began to dig my way out.

Louis and Clair sat on the floor across from me one night. Clair had dealt a hand of Rummy and I stared at the cards not really feeling the desire to play when I sighed and put them down.

"I've never loved someone like I loved him," I said and both my siblings stopped and looked at me.

"It's not like we'd known each other for a long time, but he just felt so right, you know?" I asked.

Clair got off the floor and scooted in next to me on the chair.

"It'll get better, I promise," she said.

I wanted to argue with her, but it was already getting better. It still hurt, but every day the pain was just a little less intense than it had been the day before.

Slowly, over time, I was able to get myself back together. I swore that was the last time I was putting all my trust in a man, but I had a horrible feeling if

Liam were to contact me the next day, I'd happily go crawling back to him.

Liam Rickard

I knew I couldn't stand to be in New York when Comic-Con started again. This is when we'd become what we are. Our first anniversary as a couple should've been a celebration not a time when I'd lost everything that ever mattered to me.

I rented a chateau not far from my uncle and aunt's place. After roaming the French countryside until I was sick of myself, I holed up in the chateau. After a month of feeling sorry for myself, I decided that maybe writing would have the same cathartic effect on me as it had on Bobby.

I wasn't good at it. Nothing about writing came naturally to me. I'd taken creative writing classes, of course, knowing I'd one day be in the publishing industry. I'd been awful at it then and I was awful at it now. Despite that, I fumbled until I finally just decided to write my side of the story.

I wrote about my privileged childhood and how lonely I'd been. I played on the fact that I knew I represented the pathetic poor little rich kid.

For the most part, I'd had a good childhood despite the fact that I'd never really fit into the elite crowd. I described my mom and how she flouted convention, choosing to take care of me herself, rather than delegate her responsibilities to a nanny.

I sat back in my chair and let the memories swirl around me. Smiling as I remembered how we'd spend days in the park, and when the other kids' nannies would speak to her, assuming she was a nanny as well, she'd let her French accent slip out, allowing them think she was an a*u pair* for the Rickard family. Then she and I would secretly laugh about it later.

I leaned forward, the smile falling from my face as wrote about school and how I'd been sent to high-end private schools where I'd learned that money and privilege were like tools to be wielded, not unlike a sword in battle. Those who knew how to wield them effectively would have better grades and more opportunities than those who didn't.

When it came to my father, it was much more difficult to write anything positive. I spent over a week writing down memories I had of him. When I was done, I was saddened by how little interaction he'd had with me. He'd always been more of an observer in our family than anything else, and for him, work always took priority over my mother or me. Even when I was at college, he kept his distance. Where other *protégés* to their fathers started working in the industry during their youth, my father kept me at arm's length until I was done with school.

After finishing dad's chapter, I laid down but couldn't sleep as the memories swirled through my brain. The next day I would be writing about Atticus. I didn't fight the memories of him like I usually did, allowing myself to remember how he had pursued me, being one of the first men in my life to pay attention to me.

When I finally forced myself to write about my Atticus experiences, I wrote about my confusion over why my already distant father became cold and uncommunicative. Of course, I had no idea Atticus had shown interest in my father or that my father might be interested in him.

Finally, with the hard family stuff done, or mostly done, I wrote several chapters about taking over the company when it was in a major slump after my father retired.

Before I wrote about Bobby, I had a mini-breakdown and spent several days wandering aimlessly around the countryside. As horrible as remembering Atticus and my father had been, it was nothing as painful as having to let Bobby go.

Finally, I was mentally prepared to deal with that chapter of my life. I was surprised as happiness filled me while I wrote about how Bobby Devereaux had been like a ray of sunshine after months of gray skies, and because of the success of his work, other authors began to see Rickards as a viable option for publishing their books again. I made it clear that Devereaux was the reason Rickard Publishing survived. That and the efforts of insanely gifted people like Roy Letterman, who had dedicated himself to ensuring our books represented quality authors.

I confessed to falling in love with Bobby and talked about going to his Iowa farm, falling into the big puddle of pig shit, and leaving with my pride in tatters. I confessed that I had gone there uninvited, trying to force his hand so he'd write another masterpiece because I needed to keep Rickard Publishing from collapsing again.

I wrote about how Bobby had written the second novel as an apology to me, when I had no right to ask it of him to begin with. I confessed that I was unworthy of the relationship that developed between us.

If I had been deserving of his love, I would've accepted his resolve to never write again. That said, book two and the upcoming book three were remarkable, and the world would've been missing out without them.

I didn't spare any details as I wrote about the scandal. I described how Randy and Jessie had conspired against Bobby with Atticus and convinced a critic to give him a negative review. I explained how Bobby had overcome it, not with legal action or hatred, but because his fans stood up for him, announcing to the world what a good writer he was.

After finishing Bobby's part of the book, I collapsed and didn't write for several more weeks. I missed him so much. It was like I'd never be happy again now that he was gone.

In the end, I decided I deserved to have my story heard., Jessie and Randy had all actively worked to destroy our lives, and the world should at least have the chance to hear the truth.

If forced myself once more to sit at the laptop and write. I concluded the story with how I'd been canned because of the scandal and how I'd subsequently broken things off with Bobby to protect his reputation.

I wasn't one to air my feelings. That's something I'd learned from my father. But I wanted to lay it all on the line. I wanted people to understand how much I'd lost and not just my job. That was the least of my concerns. It was losing Bobby that had destroyed my hope of ever being happy again and this book was my way of confessing my sins to the world.

I reread the autobiography, fixing errors. In editor mode, I ripped it apart, then rewrote it. By mid-summer, I was confident that the book was in good enough shape to be sent to Doug.

From: Liam
To: Doug:
Subject: Manuscript

You're the only agent I trust. Would you please read this and tell me what you think? Honest opinion.

I must have checked my emails every ten minutes until I finally heard back from him, a full week later.

From: Doug
To: Liam
Subject: Manuscript

That's one of the saddest stories I've ever read, man. What do you want me to do with it?

I told him that if he thought it was publishable to submit it to anywhere but Rickard Publishing.

I had ten offers to publish by the end of the following week. Of course, that was no surprise. All those companies would love the chance to publish a tell-all book about one of the few scandals to rock the publishing world in the last two decades.

I was about to select a publisher when Roy *and* Bobby showed up at the chateau.

My heart skipped a beat. All this time, my mind had never left him. I thought of him every night before falling asleep and he was the first person I thought about when I woke up the next morning. It was both exhilarating and surreal that he was standing in my doorway.

Roy did most of the talking but I could only see Bobby, who stayed in the background, staring back at me.

"I've been asked by the board to convince you to let us publish your autobiography," Roy told me.

I couldn't take my eyes off Bobby. Just seeing him was like a dark veil had been lifted from around me.

Roy's comment caught me off guard and pulled me out of what must've been a creepy stare I'd been casting at Bobby since he walked up to my chateau.

I scoffed. "You mean to squash it."

"No," he shook his head. "It'll be published word-for-word if you prefer that. They just don't want to have it published by a competitor."

I'd guessed they would do this, and if I was honest with myself, I'd known Doug would give a copy to Roy. I was surprised, though. Not that Rickard wanted to be the ones to publish the book, but that they were being so upfront about it. I'd expected either intimidation tactics or schmoozing.

I looked over at Bobby. "And you're here to help kick the ball over the net?" Sadness that somehow Bobby was here to support the board and not me coursed through my bloodstream.

Roy spoke before Bobby could reply. "No, he said if we wanted to publish book three—which he's yet to sign a contract for—he had to be allowed to come with me to check on you."

That got a whimper out of me as I sat heavily on an old chair.

Bobby came over and knelt in front of me.

"Are you okay?" he asked almost in a whisper.

I shook my head. "No, not for a long time," I responded honestly.

He leaned over and gently pulled me into a hug.

"I've missed you so much," he said and laid his forehead against mine. "I've read the book, and I understand why you did what you did. But my heart has never been so broken. It's been horrible."

I let a tear fall without trying to hide it. Feeling Bobby in my arms again was like taking a breath of air after being suffocated.

We clung to each other for a long time, like we were both afraid if we let go, the other would disappear forever.

When we finally separated, I turned to Roy who was staring intently at a cheap old painting on the wall.

"Come into the living room," I said. "It's warmer in there."

Once they were seated, I stoked the fire in the fireplace and sat on a chair across from them. The chateau had come furnished, but the furniture was old and worn. I hadn't had the energy or the wherewithal to manage any renovations.

As I looked around, I couldn't help smiling at the irony of my judgmental reaction to the home where Bobby had been living when we first met, given the condition of the place I was currently living in.

When Bobby looked inquisitively at me, I laughed.

"I'm sorry. For a moment I was struck by how I'd been so judgmental about you living in your old farmhouse in Iowa. Now look where I'm living." I waved my hands around me as I spoke.

He looked around then and laughed. "It's funny how things come full circle, isn't it?"

I turned to Roy then.

"What are they willing to offer?" I asked.

"First, your old job back. They'd like you to take over as CEO again. They realize they made a grave error and have been unhappy with the people they tried to replace you with since you left." I waited for him to continue. "They will give you an advance that doubles your best offer and full creative control over the book."

I was shocked. A publisher never gave full creative control to an author. It was impossible to be impartial.

"Is that all?" I asked, and Roy nodded.

As I leaned back in the chair, several springs poked me in the back, reminding me how the board had stabbed me in the back before they had heard my side of the story.

"Here's my counteroffer. I'll accept, but everyone on the board must resign within twelve months of my return. It will be staggered, of course, but they've long ago lost the creative insight to be running a board such as ours. I'll let them nominate their board replacements as the bylaws stipulate, but it isn't going to be an automatic sanctioning of their first choice. The board needs to become more relevant."

Roy cocked an eyebrow but grinned. Most everyone in the administration felt the same way about the archaic and elderly board of directors. I had been planning to begin the process of replacing them when they beat me to the punch.

"Do you think they'll even consider that?" he asked.

I chuckled.

"After they let me go, the stock climbed slightly. Since then, it's decreased by almost half. So, since they are all living on the income from their stock interest, I think it's something they'll be *very* interested in. I also think they know retribution is coming. I'd bet they're all expecting it."

Roy laughed.

"You are a powerful negotiator, we really do need you back," he said.

I sighed.

"Do I want to come back? That's the question."

Bobby sat next to me. ". I miss you every day," was all he said.

I laid my head into his neck and felt at home for the first time since Christmas.

***

Bobby didn't say much but when Roy left and he stayed, I took that as a good sign.

I quickly called mom and asked if she would bring fresh linens for Bobby to stay with me.

She did and hugged Bobby like he was the solution to a problem she'd had for a long time. In a way, I guess he was. Of course, the problem was me.

After she left, I sat down next to him and stared into the fire.

"Bobby, I'm so in love with you. It hurts having been away from you for so long," I confessed, emotions swirling inside me.

Bobby shook his head. "I don't know how to fix this, Liam. I'm not sure I'll ever get over what happened, but I wasn't lying when I said I missed you. I've missed you every day since you left, but I don't know if I can start this again."

We slept in separate rooms during the weeks we remained together in France. In fact, it took a while before we even kissed. Bobby's skittishness made sense after I'd deserted him.

After getting back to the states, I flew to Iowa and spent a few days with him. Trying to mend what I'd torn apart. Finally, one night Bobby sat down next to me and let his emotions control the conversation.

"Liam, I've never been so broken as I was after you left me. I'm not sure how to fix the hurt, but I love you so much. I want to make this work."

That night, we spent hours in each other's arms. I knew I'd hurt him. Hell, I'd hurt myself, so all I could do was hope he'd eventually let me back in.

As the weeks went by and we tried to talk through things, I finally accepted I couldn't fix this with words, too much had happened. I really had no idea how to fix it. Maybe time was the only remedy.

The following night we went to Bobby's parent's house for dinner. I doubted Bobby's family were ever cold to anyone but despite their hospitality, I felt how cautious they were of me. Yet as the meal progressed, the typical teasing and prodding returned and the initial discomfort began to wane.

That night while helping his mother clean up after dinner, she confirmed how hard things had been for Bobby. As he and his siblings finished cleaning up, she pulled me into the living room and after we both sat down, she patted my knee and said, "You'll have to give him time."

Earlier during dinner, she'd noticed how when I'd put my hand on his, he'd looked uncomfortable. So different from the naturally affectionate person he'd been before.

"I really hurt him, didn't I?"

She nodded sadly. "I've never seen him so hurt."

"If it helps, I was miserable," I said to her, and she continued nodding.

"I know, dear. I read your book."

I couldn't help but blush. "Well, that's embarrassing. For me, the whole thing came across like I'm the poor little rich kid or something."

I leaned back on the sofa and looked at her.

She put her hand over mine and said, "Rich or poor, children need love and affection. It sounds like your mom was able to give that to you, at least."

I nodded.

"I guess my dad did, too, in his own way. I wonder if his sexuality might have played a role in it?"

She sat silently for a moment, clearly choosing her words. "I'm only a little younger than your parents. It wasn't easy back in the late eighties and early nineties. I lost a high school friend to suicide after a bully outed him. In college, I had a couple of gay friends who struggled to find acceptance and we were at the University of Iowa, which even then was a pretty liberal school. It would've been difficult coming to terms with his sexuality back then."

"Yeah, but when I came out, you'd think he would've found a way to tell me, to keep me from dating a man he was clearly in love with."

She put her arm around me. "We're all human, sweetheart. I'm not giving him a free pass by any means, but if you can find it in your heart to understand how different things were then compared to now, it might help you to eventually have a relationship with him, if that's what you want, at least."

"I do. Even though we weren't as close as Bobby and his dad, I miss him."

I didn't mention that as long as he was with that asshole, I would never have anything to do with him.

That conversation was serendipitous since shortly after I came back home, my dad came back into my life. I'd recently taken the CEO position back on and was working on a project when I got notice from Irene that one of the larger stockholders had requested a meeting with me. The meeting was anonymous, which wasn't unusual. Stockholders sometimes wanted to keep their meetings private for whatever reason.

I figured it was someone who was upset that I'd stepped back into the position, so I was preparing my speech in my head about how glad I was to be back and what I had planned to help move the company forward. Irene knocked, and when I gave the okay, she led my father in and closed the door.

I stood staring at my father for several moments before I fully comprehended that he was there. He was stooped and looked a lot older than his fifty-five years. His hair had greyed, and his eyes were dull instead of the vibrant blue I was used to seeing.

"Hello, Liam. May I sit down?"

I nodded, thinking of the two compartmentalized Liams that Bobby and I had created when we were first dating. I could use that now since my father was coming to see me in my role as CEO and not as his son. I would be CEO Liam and squash the personal shit from the get-go.

"How have you been?" he asked, clearly nervous.

"I'm doing okay...now, at least. How can I help you?"

I could tell he noticed I didn't call him "Dad," which I normally would've because he slumped a bit more.

"I came to discuss my role in your life. I know I've been a coward, but you deserve some closure, and I need to face my demons and clean up the shit-storm I've tossed you and your mother into."

As CEO Liam, I could calmly sit and listen to this man apologize for what he'd done to disrupt the company, but as his son, I was screaming and throwing a temper tantrum in my mind.

"I'm not sure what you want from me. It's been over a year since you and *that man* took off together, leaving chaos in your wake. Are you wanting forgiveness, or hoping I will have forgotten what you did to me, to my boyfriend, and to Mom?" I raised my voice significantly when I added, "Not to mention what it did to this company, the authors we represent, and the people who work here. Your actions had dire consequences for a lot of people."

I paused and looked at the man who sat across from me. "You realize we are just now climbing back out of this."

He nodded, then he stood to leave.

"That's it?" Son Liam had begun to escape the cage, and I was having a lot of difficulty keeping him in it.

My father shrugged. "I don't know what to say. I've stayed away because of what I did. I do know what I did and the consequences it had on you." He sat back down and put his head in his hands. "I thought he loved me. I know that's not an excuse, but it's all I've got."

He looked back up at me, and seeing my impassive expression, sighed. "I had no idea he was involved with that Randy character or that he'd conspired with that critic to intentionally hurt your boyfriend. When the scandal broke, I had just told your mother that I was moving in with him and she initiated divorce proceedings."

He shook his head and looked back at his hands. "The son of a bitch tossed me aside less than a week later, moving in with Randy. They'd set all this up to get back at you and me and so Randy could get back at Bobby."

"Did they set up the publicity, too?"

He shook his head. "No, that was that Jessie character. He was mad because Randy had tossed him aside, so he went on the attack while relishing the limelight it gave him."

I leaned back in my chair and stared at my father for a long time, trying to settle my swarming emotions.

"I don't see how I can ever forgive you for taking him as a lover and deserting me as your son. If you'd have stood up and faced me, I probably could've worked past it, but you left it to Mom—the woman you were deserting after she stood by you knowing your sexuality—to tell me what you'd done."

He opened his mouth to speak and I held my hand up.

"I may let you back in my life, but you also have to know I'll never forget that when the board voted to fire me as CEO because of the shit storm *you* stirred up, *you* refrained from voting. That led to me being fired and set adrift at a time when it was the only fucking thing in the world I had left to hold onto."

I felt my voice shaking as I said the last part, so I leaned back and let myself calm down. My father wisely didn't respond until I got my emotions under control.

When I could finally speak again, I said, "I realized while speaking to Bobby's mom that I want you back in my life. Call me stupid, call me *naïve*, but I miss you, in spite of you being a piss-poor excuse for a father. Despite that, I would like to figure out how to have you in my life, in some form or other."

My dad sighed across from me. "I didn't get involved because I was told by several board members that it would make things worse. I trusted them. I should've trusted you instead."

The tears escaped before I could stop them and I wiped them away as casually as I could.

"That will always be your mistake. You never trusted me, and now we're left with a legacy of mistrust. Which board members told you that?" I asked.

"They told me they've all resigned, so does it matter?"

"Yes, it does because I replaced them with their own suggestions. I need to know the snakes in the grass." I told him the names of the ones I suspected, and he nodded. "Anyone else?"

He shook his head.

"Good, now I know who I can't trust."

My father cleared his throat. "Your book..."

I felt my back go rigid. Here came the chastisement I'd been expecting.

"I appreciate your being so candid. You told the truth and didn't embellish it. I appreciate that, although I deserved the sordid tale Jessie Hubbard put out."

"That's not my way," I responded, feeling offended.

"No, it's not. You're a better man than that. The truth is, you're a better man than me. I'd like to explain why I was the way I was."

I sat quietly, curious about what he had to say.

"When I was a boy, my father believed the only way to make me a man was to knock me around. He was a total ass and my mother looked the other way. She was of the same mindset. When I married your mom, she made it clear that if I ever laid a hand on our children, she'd leave me. You know your mom. She is a woman of her word."

He straightened in his seat. "After you were born, I often felt rage overcome me and recognized that at any moment I could lash out at you, the same way my father had lashed out at me. I didn't know how to keep myself from raging at you when the emotions were so big and strong and often arose over such minor offenses. So, I erased all my emotions. I numbed myself with alcohol, and when that didn't work, I switched to stronger stuff. Your mother and I stopped being intimate because, after I became addicted, I just couldn't."

My dad looked at me then and sighed. "I know you hate me for not showing you love, but I'd do it again the exact same way if it kept you safe from my anger."

I stared at him. It all made sense. I remembered the weeks when my dad would disappear and the sadness my mom would show, even though she tried to stay positive.

"Are you still using?" I asked.

He shook his head. "No, that's where I've been these past few months, in and out of rehab. Learning to function through a twelve-step program."

"Dad," I sighed, then stared at him for a moment. A huge part of me wanted to scream at him again, tell him to get lost. But what good would it do? He was a drug addict. He'd let his infatuation with a dick who'd hurt me get in the way of our relationship, but in the end, would me blowing a gasket help anything? No. I sighed inwardly. If I pushed him away I might never see him again. So, instead of raging at him, I just said, "We are all fucked up!" He chuckled a little for the first time. "You realize I had no idea?"

"You have your mom to thank for that. She's a rock. I-I miss her."

"Have you spoken to her?" I asked. I wasn't sure why, but knowing my dad was an addict instead of just an ass helped me understand his choices a little more, which helped me understand him, if not forgive him.

"No, I'm a coward. I doubt she wants to see me after Atticus."

"Well, I didn't want to see you either, but I'm glad you came by."

He looked at me, shocked. "You are?"

"Well, yeah, Dad. I am now. Don't you know how confusing this has been for me? I've always thought it was because something was wrong with me, that I'd fucked up somehow. And then finding out I'd dated someone you were in love with? That really fucks with someone, a lot!"

He shook his head. "Atticus is a piece of shit and I was, well, I was strung-out and too high to make adult decisions. That has nothing to do with you and everything to do with him and me being two massive losers."

I chuckled. "Well, you're less of a loser for coming here today."

I was crying by the time I stepped into my dad's arms, and when I pulled back, he was weeping, too.

He wiped his eyes. "I love you more than anything. Your book questioned that, but you should never question it again. It was you and regretting how I'd hurt you that got me through rehab and has kept me sober for almost six months. I may be a horrible dad, but never question that I've always loved you completely and entirely."

We held each other for a long moment.

When I pulled back and got myself together, I said, "Now, as CEO of Rickard Publishing, can I get you to write the story? You could call it *Rival Son and Father, Back Together*."

"*Prodigal Family*," he corrected. "You're better at this than I was," he said, waving around the office, the humor leaving his face.

"I think I just have less to deal with. I'm able to openly love the man I love and don't have a wife and kid I'm worried about hitting."

He nodded. "I suspect there's truth in that." He turned for the door. "I'll consider that book deal."

Before he walked out, I said, "Dad, call Mom."

He looked sad, and nodded again, then ducked out of the room.

I spun around in my chair and stared out the window until I heard Irene come in behind me and sit in the chair my father had vacated.

"You okay?" she asked.

I shook my head. "Oh, no, far, far, far from okay."

She nodded in understanding. "You know, I go to Nar-Anon. Both my parents were drug addicts. I grew up with my grandmother in Trinidad after they lost custody of me in Florida. You should come with me."

"You heard him?"

She shook her head. "No, I recognized the look of a man in rehab."

I thought for a moment. "Maybe. I could go. I just hadn't known about his addiction until now."

"You'll be surprised how much you did know after talking to others. Let me know if you want to join me.

It can be helpful as you work through the emotions. Especially if you are just figuring things out about him."

"Did you know before now?" I asked.

She shook her head. "I mean, I'll admit I suspected it, but sometimes people hide it really well. I only saw your dad on occasion, and there were times when his eyes appeared to be dilated. Once I thought I saw a needle mark on his arm, but that was just speculation. You can't blame yourself for not knowing, and you can't blame others for not telling you."

I could tell she was referring to my mom.

"These things are never easy and seldom black and white. I usually go to the meetings on Fridays, but it might be good for you to go tonight. I'll be happy to go with you."

I told her I'd think about it. However, as I sat in my chair and couldn't bring myself to call Bobby, I realized this was me repeating the same behavior from before. The behavior that caused me to break up with him instead of reaching out for his support. The thought of how I'd hurt him to the point where he'd lost that sensitive, affectionate personality propelled me, and I told Irene I wanted to join her at Nar-Anon that night after all.

If I've learned one thing, it's that I'm not alone. The more I open up, the smoother my life runs. Yes, I needed Nar-Anon and any other support I could find to help me process everything.

Knowing how important it was not to bottle feelings up comes from having an incredible man in my life. Bobby Devereaux has transformed my life and I genuinely couldn't imagine being more thankful.

Liam Rickard

Taking the CEO position back was like getting on an old, worn bicycle. I hadn't told anyone, but I only intended to stay on short term. Two years tops. Meanwhile, I was, without his knowledge, grooming Roy as my replacement. The first thing I did when I returned was to reinstate the Chief Operations Officer position that had been eliminated before my father retired.

I put Roy in that position and, as I suspected, he bloomed like a spring flower, taking on more and more of my responsibilities.

My book was met with both success and a great deal of criticism. Much of that criticism landed on my father and the board for acting on emotions instead of good sense.

Of course, we wanted that response. After an appropriate amount of time, the company announced my return, even though I'd already begun taking on the workload. When I officially stepped back into the role, stocks of Rickard Publishing began to stabilize and then climb again.

With my book's success, it was almost as if the public had taken a more personal interest in the company. Stock prices reached an all-time high when I finally announced that I would be stepping down and handing the reins to my successor, whom I had personally trained and believed in.

There was some kickback in the markets, but Roy was the type of guy who could win most people over, given enough time. I took the position of President of the Board, which meant I was still involved in the company but didn't have to show up to work every day.

I was so pleased when Roy selected Irene to replace him as COO. The woman was more than capable and would be a good alternative for CEO if he ever had to leave the position. As the old board learned the hard way, bringing outside CEOs into such a tight-knit workplace was sometimes not the best idea. We were one of those companies that needed to grow its administration from the bottom up.

Even after all the chaos, Rickard Publishing had come through it all and was better and stronger than it had been in the past three decades. That was an accomplishment that would stay with me an entire lifetime.

Epilogue: Bobby Devereaux

"Damn, Bobby. Seriously, you look great. Let's go."

"It's my fucking wedding, Eddie. Let me have one last look."

I knew maybe it was overkill if Eddie was frustrated that I was preening too much, but fuck it, it was my wedding...well, mine and Liam's.

Liam's mom swished into the room to check on me, and when she looked at me, a tear fell from her eyes.

Liam chuckled as he kissed her cheek.

"Careful, Mom, you're becoming soft-hearted."

"I know," she said as she blubbered. "It's not every day your only child marries such an amazing man.

Liam's father hadn't had a dry eye since landing in Key West. The two had grown closer since they'd worked things out. The book that Liam's dad wrote about living the life of a closeted addict had caught the attention of a lot of people. It was certainly not as popular as Liam's book had been, but it did sort of explain the troubles Liam had written about in his tell-all.

We'd decided to have the wedding in Key West. Our style had become understated elegance, and Key West certainly had that in spades.

Suzie *fucking* Freemont sang as both our fathers walked beside us toward the front of the room. Our moms joined them when we arrived in front of the minister and remained there throughout the ceremony. In my mind, it perfectly represented our commitment to family and to those we loved, as we proclaimed our love for each other.

Liam turned to me as the minister instructed him to read his vows. "You, Bobby Devereaux, inspire me, fill me with hope, and pull me out of the depths of despair. You do so just by being yourself. I'd say that you saved me, but that would be too *cliché*."

The audience laughed and he paused. "I never dreamed I'd find someone I could love this much. I look forward to waking up in the morning just so I can feel you in my arms. Even when we argue, you are kind and loving. Your respect for me has taught me how to respect myself. It seems miraculous to me that I stand here in this beautiful place, committing myself to you for life. Thank you for giving this relationship to me."

When the minister turned to me, I had to take a few deep breaths to overcome the emotion that had swept over me as I heard Liam's words.

When I finally got myself together enough to speak, I looked at the audience and said, "Yeah, what he said."

When the laughter died down, I looked at the minister and said, "Time out, I need to do this real quick."

I leaned over and kissed Liam. When I regained my balance, I recited my vows. "You're my light and my inspiration. My entire life has been altered and is so much better because of you. But more importantly, you've become a part of me, so much so that without you, I'd no longer recognize myself. These past years have been the best of my life. Not every moment has been good, but even when things were hard, as long as you were with me, I was happy, happier than I've ever been. When I wake up, you're the first thing I reach for, and when I go to sleep, you're the last thing I feel. I continue to learn more about you every day, and when we are apart, I feel like there is an empty space inside me that doesn't fill up until I'm with you again. I don't care where we are, as long as you are with me."

When I almost kissed him again, the minister cleared his throat and said, "No more unauthorized kissing, young man."

The audience snickered.

"With the power vested in me by the state of Florida, Bobby Devereaux, Liam Rickard, I now pronounce you husbands. Now, young man, you may kiss your spouse!"

Liam pulled me toward him and laid a lip-lock on me that melted my insides. Funny, after four years, how he still had the power to do that. The minister cleared his throat and Liam pulled back, blushing.

When the audience tittered behind us, the minister whispered, "You must really have the hots for this guy."

The reception was amazing, mostly because it was about hanging out and partying with the people we loved. Sabastian and Eddie had gotten married the year before and fought like dogs but fiercely loved each other. They'd flown down to dress us and do our hair, determined to do their part. The fact that they now ran a very exclusive wedding venue in New York, and the two of us were still a favorite topic of gossip there, helped motivate them to take on our wedding. We were appreciative, whatever the motivation.

Suzie and Indi had become good friends of ours over the years. Suzie was rambunctious and down-to-earth, and I'd come to love her like a sister.

She and Indi had two girls, and she was semi-retired from the stage. What the rest of the world didn't know was that she was co-writing a #MeToo inspired musical for the stage that sort of followed her life and the chaos she encountered after she'd been dragged through the mud by a jackass politician. Liam and I may or may not have been co-writing it with her.

Liam had become close friends with Aiden Fisher, and we occasionally flew out to Spokane and drove down to his and Devin's east Washington ranch. Devin and I had more in common, and he would let me work the cattle, which was something I'd never done before. I'd even dragged my brother and his wife out there once, just so Louis could get away for a romantic weekend with his wife, which, incidentally, is how I ended up with a brand-new niece.

Aiden and Devin both thought that piece of information was hilarious and called the baby Little Lady Ronde after the river that flowed along the border of their property.

If we'd had a traditional wedding, Roy and Doug would've been our best men. They had been by our side the entire time our relationship had been forming. Roy was CEO of the company, and Irene was his COO. As president of the board, Liam had to threaten to fire them both if they didn't come to the wedding. Even then, they grudgingly attended, having become workaholics.

Tiffany was in charge of taking their phones away from them before the service began, and they weren't allowed to have them back until after the reception. As we walked past them, I could tell they were both sweating bullets. Doug and Cliff, Irene's husband, both looked rather smug, however, enjoying watching their spouses detached from their digital umbilical cords.

Liam surprised me by purchasing the French villa he'd stayed in during our breakup, saying it was my wedding present. It was in worse condition than when Liam had lived there, so I wasn't sure why he thought I'd want it. But it turned out that his mom had taken charge of the renovation, and with the help of his uncle and aunt who supervised the workers, it had turned out beautifully rustic, just like a French villa should be.

The villa also had a beautiful barn that was built in the early 1800s. Tiffany had decided to spend most of her time in Europe and since Liam and I spent most of our time in the states, and we needed someone to keep an eye on the villa, we let her talk us into redoing the barn when the villa was done.

It became a beautiful combination guest house and meeting space that was used by Tiffany and our friends from the States to stay when they visited her. More than a few conversations were had there, mini conventions, discussions about fundraisers, events, and political strategies to improve the planet's health.

It was almost as if my third novel's storylines came to life in that old barn. Of course, we ended up naming the place The Heroine's Lair, and it was featured multiple times in various novels and graphic novels I wrote, starring my popular heroes and heroines.

I found out that I loved writing. Funny thing was, so did my husband. He preferred non-fiction and, go figure, I only liked writing fiction. It's strange how life sometimes works out.

Life isn't always happily ever after. Sometimes it's tough. But, if my life had a theme, it was that it flows much better when you're surrounded by those you love.

***

Continue Reading for an excerpt from
Love By Chance

***

Curious about Suzie's story? Read
Suzie Empowered
Suzie struggles to overcome her past when her perpetrator returns intent on silencing her. Can she overcome her hatred and save her new relationship?

blakeallwood.com/booklink/2012694

LOVE BY CHANCE

Blake Allwood

Martin

I woke to the smell of onions and garlic frying. That was the most luscious smell in the world. I leaned up, stretching to see who was putting such an amazing aroma into the world. When I saw Elian cooking, both my heart and my groin lurched a bit. There were fewer things sexier to me than a hot man cooking in his kitchen.

Elian apparently knew what he was doing. It was clear that his sister had a knack for cooking, but I'd assumed Elian didn't. I self-reflected, realizing maybe I didn't think a man could be both business-minded and have the artistic techniques to create a good meal. Despite my prejudice against the businessman, the smells of onion and garlic certainly were a step in the right direction, and even if the food wasn't very good, the beautiful man was definitely good enough to eat.

Crap! I swore in my head, catching myself thinking of Elian as beautiful. Okay, truth be told, he was sexy as hell, but I quickly stamped my thoughts down. *No need going there. I'm spending the night alone with this man tonight, and we have an agreement to keep things business and platonic. Remember, platonic,* I reminded myself.

I stood up and walked into the kitchen. Elian looked over and flashed me that gorgeous smile of his. "I hope you're getting hungry. I decided to cook for you myself tonight instead of parading you through the city. Hopefully, you'll go easy on me since I'm not a pro like my sister is." He turned to put the marinated beef into the pan with the garlic and onions.

"I never complain when a man cooks for me. It is one of my favorite sights in the world. I'd rather see that than a stripper," I said with a self-conscious laugh.

Elian cocked an eyebrow at me, then hummed a stripping song, pretending to strip and flip the meat all at the same time.

"You are a goof," I said, teasing him. But the silly act had done more than a little to turn me on. Had things been different, I was almost sure poor Elian would have burned his meal after I did some of the things I was imagining to his body... things that involved him continuing with that sexy little dance.

I shook my head and turned to go back to the living room, giving myself time to clear the thoughts of bedding Elian out of my mind. As I turned, I asked, "So, what was the outcome of your meeting?"

Elian shook his head. "The bartender was inherited from the previous owner. In fact, I think they were having an affair. When the previous owner sold to me, she broke it off with him. Apparently, he's been using his position at the bar to get even with me. At least that is how he put it before he threw the bar towel at me and stomped out yelling he quit."

"He was deliberately sabotaging you?" I asked.

"It appears so," Elian replied. "Too bad, too, because he came highly recommended, and when he served *me* a drink, they were always top-notch."

"What are you going to do?" I asked.

"The manager has called in a favor from a man she used to work with. He is going to cover until we can find a bartender who doesn't want to chase off all our customers."

"I'm sorry that happened," I sighed.

"I'm just glad I had you come out this weekend. If we can fix this fast enough, I think we will save our bar business. I am going to be comping a lot of drinks for the next few weeks to build back our reputation," Elian sighed.

I nodded. "I think giving away a few good drinks to your repeat customers is a very good idea. Don't be surprised, though, if you have several people decline. You may need to make sure your wait staff is telling everyone you have a new barkeep. In fact, that could be the excuse for offering a free drink."

"Clever," Elian replied thoughtfully.

I yawned big and raised my arms over my head, causing my stomach to show under my shirt. When I glanced back at Elian, his face had gone from platonic to something very, *very* different.

"Um, where do you work out at?" he stammered.

I looked at him and, with a cocked eyebrow, asked, "Where did that come from?"

Elian blushed. "I noticed your abs when you were yawning," he replied. His face continued to turn a darker red from the awkward question.

I was enjoying the effect my stomach was having on Elian. The man seemed unflappable, but a little skin seemed to completely undo him. Yet, watching the man's reaction caused something to snap inside me as well. I'd been resisting my urge to kiss this guy since he'd showed up this morning, and his flustered awkwardness was the last straw.

I walked over to where he was cooking. Elian watched me with ever-widening eyes. I lifted my shirt over my abs, and then took it completely off. "I've been working out. All that restaurant food was going to turn me into a slob. What do you think?"

Elian gulped, and I chuckled low in my throat. "So, when is dinner going to be done?" I whispered in his ear.

"Um," was all Elian was able to get out, then he swallowed hard enough for me to hear.

"What?" I decided to play coy. "I just wanted to show you how I like to work out."

Again, Elian stammered but flipped off the heat under the pan. I laughed again, enjoying seeing this guy turned to mush over my body. I reached over and put my shirt back on, then leaned into Elian and kissed him square on the mouth.

"It is good to see you are as turned on by me as I am by you," I said, "but that doesn't mean we're going to do anything, Elian Whitman."

As I turned to leave, Elian spun me back around and kissed me deep and hard. This time, there was no civil peck; the kiss Elian gave possessed all the angst between us these past weeks. If I was going to pull back, it was going to have to be soon because Elian had just lifted the kiss to another level: tongue, saliva, and pure sexuality rolled into me like a storm surge in a category five hurricane.

Within an instant, my shirt was back off, and Elian's came off shortly after. We crossed the room, our kisses growing more passionate and desperate. Elian pushed me onto the sofa, and began assaulting my neck, then chest, and paused when he got to my nipples to nip ever so slightly. This was going to be raw sexuality, and Elian wasn't holding anything back.

Deep in the recesses of my mind, I could hear a faint cry from the part of my brain that told me to watch out—not to get close to a man again. *Especially this man, keep him at bay.* But instead of listening to that voice—which was just a little too easy to ignore—I responded to the need that Elian poured onto me.

***

To purchase Love By Chance, go to
blakeallwood.com/booklink/2035955

To stay up to date on all of Blake's new releases, join his mailing list at:
blakeallwood.com

***

Looking for more books by #ownvoice authors?

Check out

lgbtqownvoice.com